The Illinois Detective Agency: The Case of the Stalking Moon

The Illinois Detective Agency: The Case of the Stalking Moon

BOOK 2

Ethan J. Wolfe

FIVE STAR
A part of Gale, a Cengage Company

Five Star Publishing, a part of Gale, a Cengage Company

LIBRARY OF CONGRESS CATALOGING-IN-PUBLICATION DATA

Names: Wolfe, Ethan J., author.
Title: The case of the stalking moon / Ethan J Wolfe.
Description: First edition. | [Waterville] : Five Star, [2021] | Series: The Illinois Detective Agency ; 2
Identifiers: LCCN 2021014158 | ISBN 9781432883171 (hardcover)
Subjects: GSAFD: Mystery fiction. | Western stories.
Classification: LCC PS3612.A5433 C36 2021 | DDC 813/.6—dc23
LC record available at https://lccn.loc.gov/2021014158

First Edition. First Printing: December 2021
Find us on Facebook—https://www.facebook.com/FiveStarCengage
Visit our website—http://www.gale.cengage.com/fivestar
Contact Five Star Publishing at FiveStar@cengage.com

Printed in Mexico
Print Number: 01 Print Year: 2022

For Marjolein

Prologue

Dan Tyrell and Mike Poe were as nervous as an abandoned cat stuck in a well as they made camp for the night.

They enjoyed their jobs as hands for the Foster Ranch and usually didn't mind working overnight shifts on the range. It gave them the chance to get away from the hard pace of a cowboy's life and relax in the outdoors. Besides, Foster always added a little something extra to their thirty-dollars-a-month pay for their trouble.

Tonight was different.

As they set up camp, both men were jumpy, skittish, and just plain nervous.

Poe built a fire as Tyrell tended to their horses. They cooked a supper of beans with chunks of beef and bacon and hunks of cornbread on the side and coffee. Poe added a few ounces of whiskey to the pot for flavor and a splash to the coffee.

They ate as the sun set and darkness enveloped them.

"What do you think?" Poe said.

"I think the hundred cows we're babysitting will alert us to any danger," Tyrell said. "And our horses. Cows and horses sense danger better than people. A horse knows the rattler is there before you even see it. I think we'll sleep in shifts until morning, just in case."

"Good idea," Poe said.

After supper, they sat against their saddles with cups of whiskey-laced coffee and rolled cigarettes.

"Moon's up," Poe said.

"Don't think about it," Tyrell said.

"How can I not think about it?" Poe said. "It's a full moon, staring me in the face."

"That don't mean something is going to happen just because it's a full moon," Tyrell said. "Let's play a hand of cards for first watch."

Poe lost the hand and drew first watch. He borrowed Tyrell's pocket watch and, as Tyrell slept from eight to ten o'clock, he kept watch over the herd and their lives. He kept busy feeding the fire and by checking the herd, even though the ladies were tucked in for the night.

At ten, he woke Tyrell, gave him his watch back, and grabbed some sleep.

Tyrell spent the next two hours feeding the fire, smoking rolled cigarettes, and reading a ten-cent western novel.

At midnight, he woke Poe and went back to sleep.

Around one in the morning, Poe went to relieve himself. When he returned, Tyrell was dead in his bedroll.

Scalped.

Poe drew his sidearm and scanned the camp.

He never saw the tomahawk that took his scalp and his life.

In the morning, Foster dispatched his foreman, John Banks, to the west range to have Tyrell and Poe move the herd to the north range where the grass was more plentiful.

Banks was horrified at the sight that greeted him.

CHAPTER ONE

Charles Porter, the founder and owner of the Illinois Detective Agency in Springfield, Illinois, puffed on a long Cuban cigar as he entertained the governor of Wyoming Territory.

The governor, William Hale, had been appointed by President Chester Arthur two years earlier, in 1882.

"I'm telling you, Charles, the army can't seem to do anything about it, and there aren't enough marshals to cover the territory. Two weeks ago, two more cowboys were scalped and murdered during the night of the full moon. That makes at least one such incident every month since January."

"There haven't been any uprisings on the reservations in years in Wyoming Territory that I'm aware of," Porter said.

"The Indian Affairs agent, escorted by army troops, has visited the reservations," Hale said. "The chiefs all claim no knowledge of a renegade committing these ghastly murders."

Porter sighed. "Are you staying in town tonight?" he said.

"At the Springfield Hotel," Hale said. "I'll catch my train home in the morning."

"Let me talk to my people, and I'll meet you for dinner at, say, seven o'clock at your hotel," Porter said.

"Very good, Charles," Hale said.

After Hale left the office, Porter reached for the cone on his desk. The cone was attached to a hose that went under the floor and surfaced at the desk of his secretary, Miss Potts. Her end also had a cone she could speak to Porter through. Talk was that the telephone lines would come to Springfield in a few years. Porter hoped to have one installed as soon as he was able.

"Miss Potts?" Porter said into the cone. "A moment, please."

"Yes, sir," she replied.

A few moments later, Miss Potts opened the office door and entered the office.

"Mr. Porter?" she said.

"Agents Duffy and Cavill, where are they?" Porter said.

"At the moment, each is visiting his sweetheart," Miss Potts said.

"Good grief," Porter said. "Who said they could do that?"

"You did," Miss Potts said. "They were exhausted after their last assignment. You thought a rest would do them some good."

"Remind me not to do that again," Porter said.

"I'll make a note," Miss Potts said.

"Who isn't engaged at the moment?" Porter said.

"Joe Charles and Tom Adcock are home from their last assignment," Miss Potts said.

"Send for them and tell them to be in the office at nine sharp tomorrow morning," Porter said. "No, on second thought, tell them to meet me for dinner at the Springfield Hotel at seven. Tell them to dress."

"Very good, sir," Miss Potts said.

"Is Goodluck at his desk?" Porter said.

"I believe so," Miss Potts said. "Shall I send for him?"

"No, I need to stretch my legs," Porter said. "And maybe you should attend dinner with us and bring your notepad."

"Yes, Mr. Porter," Miss Potts said.

Joseph Goodluck, born of a Mexican mother and Comanche father fifty years earlier, had been many things. A warrior, a father and husband, a horse wrangler and brander, a scout for the army, and now a detective for Porter's agency.

When Mr. Porter offered him a job after he worked with Cavill and Duffy on a cattle theft case, he took the job for the added money. He sent his pay to the reservation. He didn't mind the white man's clothes so much and really liked their food. He thought he would hate living in their houses, but he enjoyed indoor plumbing very much. He thought he would be bored working in an office, but he found the work fascinating.

Especially the assignment he was working on now. Porter had the idea that if you took every known criminal and outlaw's photograph or sketch and their history and put them all together in one book, it would help sheriffs, marshals, and city police identify wanted men much quicker than they could using wanted posters.

One recent afternoon, when Porter brought him the latest batch of photographs, Goodluck casually remarked, "What an ugly mug on this one."

Porter said, "That's it. I've been wondering what to call the book and that's what we'll call it: a mug book."

When the book was complete, Porter planned to take it before Congress in Washington.

"Mr. Goodluck," Porter said as he entered Goodluck's office.

"Yes, Mr. Porter," Goodluck said.

"Go home and change into a suit," Porter said. "We're having dinner with the governor of Wyoming at seven tonight."

Chapter Two

"Mr. Charles, Mr. Adcock, Mr. Goodluck, this is William Hale, Governor of Wyoming Territory," Porter said when they were seated at a private table in the VIP room. "And I believe you already met Miss Potts, my personal secretary."

"Good evening to you all," Hale said.

"Let's order and then the governor can tell you his problem," Porter said.

After ordering, Hale cleared his throat with a sip of water. "It began six months ago in late January during the full moon," he said. "Two farmers, brothers trying to make a go of a small homestead, were scalped and murdered during the full moon."

"Scalped?" Adcock said.

"For three nights under the full moon, men and women were scalped and butchered," Hale said. "Then, as the moon waned, the butchering stopped. At first we thought it a lone incident, but it's happened every full moon for the past six months, including two weeks ago."

As he spoke, Miss Potts took notes in shorthand, a series of abbreviated letters to save time and space on paper.

"The ranchers, farmers, and citizens of Wyoming are living in fear," Hale said. "And this renegade must be stopped before the next full moon."

"How sure are you it's a renegade?" Adcock said.

"Who else would kill using just a tomahawk?" Hale said. "And he has the ability to sneak up on his victims sight unseen.

Who else could it be but a renegade?"

"Adcock and Charles are two of my top men in the field and Joseph Goodluck was the best scout in the army for more than a decade," Porter said. "I'm sending them to Cheyenne to gather full reports and documentation before starting a plan of action. Is that agreeable to you, Governor?"

"Yes," Hale said. "I'll have documentation and reports on all the incidents since January to now and also put the army, county sheriffs, and marshals on alert that you're coming and will be investigating on my behalf."

The waiter arrived with dinner and the table talk turned lighter while they ate. Porter told a few stories of the old days when he was a young cattle detective in Wyoming, Utah, and Montana, where he had to battle not just cattle thieves but hostile Indian tribes.

After dinner, dessert was coffee and pie.

"Before we retire for brandy and cigars, Miss Potts, would you care to join us or take a taxi home?" Porter said.

"When have you ever witnessed me drink brandy and smoke a cigar?" Miss Potts said.

"I'll escort you to the lobby and get you a taxi," Goodluck said.

After Goodluck and Potts left the room, Hale said, "Charles, he is half Comanche, isn't he?"

"If you're worried about that, he scouted for the army, for Greene and Gatewood, and helped round up Geronimo on more than one occasion," Porter said. "He's a very good man, Bill. I'm lucky to have him."

"Let's have our brandy and cigars," Hale said.

In the gentlemen's room at the hotel, Porter passed out the cigars he brought with him and a waiter poured brandy.

The cigars were imported from Cuba and cost a dollar and

twenty-five cents apiece.

"Governor Hale, I am curious as to what evidence has been gathered from each incident?" Adcock said.

"Evidence?" Hale said. "Besides the scalped and murdered victims?"

"All of my men undergo training in modern forensics, Governor," Porter said. "There is far more than meets the eye to a crime scene than just a body."

"I'll leave that to you experts," Hale said. "My concern is putting a stop to these murders and moving Wyoming closer to statehood."

"That reminds me, Bill, how is that thing going with Yellowstone?" Porter said.

"Montana is still claiming Yellowstone belongs to them, but by God I won't allow them to steal it from Wyoming," Hale said.

"If there is anything I can do," Porter said.

"I appreciate that, Charles," Hale said. "Now, let's talk about what your services are going to cost me."

Chapter Three

In the morning, dressed in casual suits, Adcock, Charles, and Goodluck stood before Porter's desk as he counted out ten-thousand dollars in expense money.

"Your gear is packed and your horses drawn from the stable?" Porter said.

Porter owned a stable that housed forty horses, used by his agents as necessary.

"All ready to go," Adcock said.

Porter handed the expense money to Adcock, who placed it into a long, leather wallet.

"Where is Miss Potts?" Porter said.

"At her desk," Goodluck said.

Porter picked up the cone. "Miss Potts, do you have the railroad tickets?"

"On my desk," Miss Potts replied.

"After you meet with the governor, wire me your plan of action," Porter said.

"Don't worry, we will," Charles said.

"And please be discreet," Porter said. "The good people of Wyoming Territory are already in a panic as it is."

"We will, sir," Adcock said.

"Good luck," Porter said. "Pick up your railroad tickets on the way out. And get receipts for the expense money whenever possible."

At her desk, Miss Potts gave Charles the three round-trip

railroad tickets.

"Good luck, men. And God bless," Miss Potts said.

Adcock, Charles, and Goodluck left the office and walked to the stables and mounted their horses. Charles and Adcock didn't own a horse and used two from the forty Porter owned. Goodluck had his own horse, which had served him well for the last eight years.

They rode to the railroad depot where their luggage was already in a carriage owned by Porter and driven by one of the stable managers.

"Where are you men off to?" the stable manager said.

"Cheyenne," Adcock said.

"Best of luck," the stable manager said.

"That's the third person to wish us good luck this morning," Charles said. "How can our assignment fail?"

"I can think of a hundred ways," Goodluck said.

They boarded the horses in the boxcar, then carried their luggage and gear into the train to their sleeper cars.

Then they met in a riding car and waited for the train to leave the depot. Finally, it rolled out, picked up speed, and they were underway.

A conductor came through to punch tickets.

"When does the dining car open for breakfast?" Adcock asked him.

"In ten minutes for coffee, thirty minutes for breakfast," the conductor said.

"Let's get some coffee," Adcock said.

As they ate breakfast, Adcock said, "Goodluck, what do you make of this situation?"

Goodluck took a sip of coffee to wash down a piece of toast. "Are you asking because I work for Mr. Porter, or because I'm half Comanche, or because I was an army scout, or all three?"

"Maybe a bit of all three," Adcock said.

"As a young man, it wasn't too out of the ordinary for a warring tribe to take scalps," Goodluck said. "After the pacification program and the scalp hunters were hired to . . ."

"I'm not familiar with the scalp hunters program," Charles said.

"The government paid five dollars each for the scalps of Indians not living on a reservation," Goodluck said.

Charles and Adcock stared at Goodluck.

"It wasn't exactly America's finest hour," Goodluck said. "But to get to the point, it would take one pissed-off Comanche or Apache or Cheyenne to take scalps in this modern world."

"Pissed off about what?" Adcock said.

"Have you ever been to a reservation?" Goodluck said.

"No," Adcock said.

"Every treaty since 1836 has been broken by your government," Goodluck said. "The Indians live on the reservations because they are a beaten people and have nowhere else to go in the land that once belonged to them. So they farm and they hunt and they live in cabins, and war is no longer a way of life for them. But is a Comanche, Apache, or Cheyenne still capable of doing this? Absolutely."

"But why?" Adcock said.

Goodluck took a sip of coffee and then smiled. "That is what we're going to Wyoming to find out, isn't it?" he said. "The why."

"Let's go to the gentlemen's car and play cards or something," Charles said.

It wasn't yet nine o'clock in the morning and the gentlemen's car was empty when Charles, Adcock, and Goodluck entered.

Adcock and Charles took a table by the window and played cards. Goodluck returned to his room for a book he had started to read, titled *Twenty Thousand Leagues Under the Sea.* Then he returned to the gentlemen's car and sat quietly beside a window and opened the book.

Goodluck removed the leather cigar holder from his jacket pocket and lit a cigar with a wood match.

"Hey, Goodluck, that looks like one of Porter's cigars," Adcock said.

"It is," Goodluck said. "He gave me a box of his Cuban cigars as a gift when I took the job. I've been saving them for just such an assignment."

Charles looked at Adcock. "I didn't get a box of cigars. Did you?"

"No," Adcock said.

"Deal the cards," Charles said.

By ten-thirty, the car had filled to near capacity, and Charles and Adcock had four additional players at their table in a penny-bet game.

Frustrated by the many conversations around him, Goodluck left the car and went to his sleeper car to continue reading.

By one o'clock, Charles had won eleven hands and lost seventeen, Adcock had won fourteen hands and lost the like amount, and they bowed out of the game in time for lunch.

They returned to their sleeper cars to freshen up, and then met Goodluck in the dining car.

Joe Charles was thirty-seven years old and originally from New Jersey. He hated the East. Rather than spend his life living in a crowded city and working in a factory, he enlisted in the army at the age of eighteen just as the Civil War was coming to a close. He was sent to Georgia to help with Reconstruction, and then to Fort Dodge in Kansas. In all, he spent eight years in the army before retiring as a sergeant. He decided to stay out west and worked as a sheriff in several towns in Kansas,

Nebraska, and Utah before finding work for Charles Porter as an agent.

Tom Adcock, also thirty-seven years old, never served in the army. He was born in Utah to a Mormon family and hated their way of life. He ran away at the age of eighteen and went to Chicago, where he went to school and later worked as a policeman. He excelled at the job, but after being shot by a criminal during an arrest, he was forced to retire in order to recover. While still recovering, he was recruited by Porter, and went to work for him as an agent.

Paired for the past few years, Charles and Adcock worked well together on many assignments. Both men were confirmed bachelors with no interest in marriage, or at least until after they retired from service. Both men were frugal with their money and saved most of their pay. They lived in a boardinghouse near the office, which cost them twenty-five dollars a month. They saved most of what they earned. They planned, once they retired from service, to pool their money and open a business in Chicago.

Over lunch, Charles said, "Goodluck, what is that book you are reading?"

"It's by Jules Verne, a Frenchman who writes stories about science-themed adventures," Goodluck said.

"I never heard of him," Adcock said.

"You can read it when I'm finished," Goodluck said.

They ordered baked chicken for lunch.

"I've been thinking about our assignment," Charles said. "About this renegade. Why only on the full moon does he kill? Why isn't he out there all the time if he is truly a renegade with a grudge?"

"I was wondering that, too," Adcock said. "What is it about a full moon that brings him out?"

"Assuming it has anything to do with the moon, it could be

any number of reasons known just to him," Goodluck said. "A family member could have been murdered under a full moon. It could be a spiritual reason. It could be why wolves and pumas are more successful when hunting under a full moon, because they can see better at night."

"Well, shit. I guess we'll just have to wait and see for ourselves," Charles said.

"That's usually how it goes," Goodluck said.

After a decent night's sleep, Goodluck met Adcock and Charles for breakfast at eight.

By nine-thirty, the train arrived in Cheyenne. They retrieved their horses and luggage and walked to the hotel on Main Street to check into a room and board their horses.

Adcock and Charles had a shave and all three a bath. Then, wearing clean suits, they took a horse taxi to the governor's office in the capital.

Chapter Four

Governor Hale greeted them in his office, where they moved to a long conference table. A large stack of reports rested beside a coffee pot and cups.

An aide poured the coffee and then quietly left the room.

Once everyone was seated, Hale said, "I'll be honest with you men; the situation here in Wyoming is not good, not good at all. Farmers, homesteaders, and ranchers are pulling up stakes and moving out by the dozens over these murders and scalpings. Talk of statehood is on hold because of it. Washington wants population, commerce, and successful ranchers and farmers before the people are allowed to vote on statehood. Throw in the dispute with Montana over Yellowstone, and statehood could be put off for another decade."

Goodluck looked at the stack of reports. "All these concern the killings?" he said.

"From sheriffs, marshals, and the army," Hale said. "Some are from witnesses."

"Witnesses?" Adcock said. "You mean some people claim they saw him in the act?"

"Either before or after," Hale said.

"Governor, I think what we should do before we decide a course of action is to read all these reports," Goodluck said.

"I agree," Hale said. "My secretary has typed up the reports and will give you copies to take with you. Read them, formulate a plan, and then report back to me. Is two days enough time?"

"We'll see you in two days, Governor," Charles said.

The detectives worked in Adcock's room at the desk in the corner. They requested a table be brought in, and they used it to spread out the reports by dates.

Then they sent for a pot of coffee and started reading reports.

In January, under the first full moon of the new year, two cowboys working as linemen for a ranch near the Bighorn Mountains were scalped and murdered during the night as they slept in their beds.

In February, three lineman working for a ranch west of the Yellowstone River were attacked during the night as they nursed a sick calf in the barn. Two were scalped and murdered. The third managed to hide in the barn loft and survived. He described the attacker as an Indian and a giant.

March saw two farmers scalped in their beds as they slept. They were brothers trying to make a go of a small homestead.

April saw two cowboys scalped as they slept in their bedrolls after driving a herd of cattle.

In May, three cowboys driving a herd from Yellowstone to Cheyenne were the next victims. One cowboy left camp to bring up the drags, and when he returned to camp, his two partners lay scalped and murdered in their bedrolls. Under the light of the full moon, the third cowboy described the person he saw riding away as a giant.

Adcock, Charles, and Goodluck worked until well after midnight before retiring.

In the morning, they returned to work right after breakfast and continued reading reports until they broke for lunch.

They ate in the hotel dining room.

"What do we have so far?" Adcock said. "A few witnesses who claim they saw a giant Indian. Sheriff reports that are useless. Reports from marshals that state they investigated and found nothing. Dozens of reports from the army that state they could not track this giant to any source."

"The Foster Ranch is only a hundred miles north of here," Goodluck said. "Since it's where the latest killing occurred, why not start there and work our way west?"

"Let's see the governor," Charles said.

"Ben Foster's place is a two and a half days' ride north of here on the North Platte River," Hale said. "It's an above-average-size spread, and he produces a good two thousand head a year. He's the kind of man Wyoming can't afford to lose."

"Is he pulling up stakes?" Adcock said.

"When he came to see me last week, the matter was discussed," Hale said. "Foster came to Wyoming twenty-five years ago when it was a lawless place filled with outlaws, cutthroats, and Indians hell-bent on killing every white man they saw. He survived by his wits and made a solid ranch and name for himself. He's young enough to run for the state senate when Wyoming is admitted to the union. Men like Foster are a rare, dying breed we cannot afford to lose."

"We'll talk to him, Governor," Charles said.

"The railroad doesn't have a route north to his ranch just yet, so you'll have to ride the hundred miles," Hale said.

"We have good horses, Governor," Goodluck said.

"We'll leave in the morning after we draw supplies," Charles said.

"Best of luck, men," Hale said.

On the way out, Goodluck said, "We should send a wire to Mr. Porter with our plans."

After dinner, Adcock, Charles, and Goodluck took coffee on the front porch of the hotel. It was a warm night, and they left their jackets in their rooms.

Goodluck lit a Cuban cigar.

"How are those?" Adcock said.

Goodluck handed Adcock and Charles a cigar. They lit up and puffed thick clouds of smoke.

"This is much better than the nickel crappers I usually smoke," Adcock said.

"We should have brandy instead of coffee," Charles said.

"Porter doesn't approve of drinking while on assignment," Adcock said.

"That reminds me. We should check in the morning for a reply from Mr. Porter," Goodluck said.

"Yeah," Adcock said.

"Goodluck, what do you make of the witness reports of him being a giant?" Charles said.

"I stand five-foot-eight-inches tall," Goodluck said. "How tall are you?"

"Five-eleven," Adcock said.

"Ever stood next to Jack Cavill?" Goodluck said. "Some people call him a giant."

"Point taken," Adcock said.

"I'm going to bed," Goodluck said. "We have an early start in the morning."

Chapter Five

The road north out of Cheyenne was well-worn, having been carved out by freight wagons over two decades.

By noon of the second day, Adcock, Charles, and Goodluck had covered fifty of the one-hundred-mile trip to the Foster Ranch.

They stopped to eat a hot lunch of beans, bacon, cornbread, and coffee. As they ate, a freight wagon passing by stopped. The detectives offered the two men in the wagon cups of hot coffee.

"Where you headed?" one of the drivers said.

"Foster Ranch," Adcock said.

"Ben Foster?" the driver said.

"You know him?" Charles said.

"Been making deliveries to him for years," the driver said.

Charles held up his wallet, which displayed his identification as a detective. "We've been employed by Governor Hale to investigate the recent murders that take place under the full moon. We're on our way to see Mr. Foster right now. Have you heard anything about these doings?"

"Enough to know to stay indoors with a loaded shotgun by my side when the moon is up," the driver said. "Well, thanks for the coffee."

After dark, having traveled eighty miles in two days, Charles, Adcock, and Goodluck make camp and prepared a supper of beef stew with fresh vegetables, bread, and coffee.

Adcock added some bourbon to the stew for flavor.

By the light from the campfire, Goodluck studied a local map.

"If we get an early start and push hard, we'll reach the Foster Ranch by noon," Goodluck said.

"No sense posting guards tonight," Adcock said. "The full moon isn't for six nights. We'll leave before sunup."

They reached the Foster Ranch a bit before one in the afternoon after being delayed a bit when Adcock's horse threw a shoe. Fortunately, Goodluck always traveled with at least six extra shoes in his gear, so it wasn't much of a problem.

There was a turnoff in the road with a sign that read *Foster Ranch.*

As they traveled the dirt road to the main house, they passed two fenced-in ranges with hundreds of cattle grazing in the sun, but they saw no cowboys.

When they reached the main house, Ben Foster and his daughter, Amelia, were seated in chairs on the porch, drinking lemonade. Foster was a lean man in his fifties with graying hair.

"Mr. Foster, you have a beautiful spread here," Adcock said.

"Honey, get the men some cold lemonade," Foster said.

Amelia stood and went inside the house.

"Grab a seat, men, you must be tired from the ride," Foster said.

Adcock, Charles, and Goodluck took chairs on the porch.

"I'll be honest with you, boys," Foster said. "I have a buyer for the ranch. He'll pay me forty thousand for the whole shebang, and I'm considering it. I'm fifty-six now and I don't have the strength I once did. Eight of my twelve hands have quit after what happened three weeks ago. If more murders happen anywhere else in the territory the next full moon, I'll lose the rest."

Amelia returned with a tray and three glasses of lemonade.

"I hope you choose not to sell, Mr. Foster," Charles said. "The governor speaks very highly of you."

"The governor isn't going to drive my heard to Cheyenne, and the governor isn't going to protect my daughter should this savage return in five nights looking for more blood," Foster said.

"Mr. Foster, can we see where the cowboys were murdered?" Goodluck said.

"I'll saddle my horse," Foster said.

"I'll go with you," Amelia said.

The west range was the closest to the house. The ride took about forty minutes. A good four-hundred head of cattle roamed freely on the range, unguarded by a single cowboy.

"My foreman, John Banks, discovered the bodies near the fire in the morning," Foster said.

They dismounted at the cold campfire pit.

Goodluck got down on one knee to inspect the dirt and soft earth.

"Boot prints," Goodluck said. "Two sets belonging to the cowboys. One set belonging to your foreman. The fourth set of prints belongs to who?"

"What are you talking about?" Foster said.

"See the prints belonging to your two cowboys? Coming and going around the camp, leading to and away from their horses," Goodluck said. "These here belong to your foreman. His horse was here and he dismounted here. See?"

Adcock, Charles, Foster, and Amelia looked closely at the footprints.

"This fourth set of tracks shows moccasin prints coming from the north. They belong to who?" Goodluck said. "I doubt your hands wear moccasins to sleep."

"Son of a bitch," Foster said.

Goodluck mounted his horse and followed the fourth set of prints. Adcock, Charles, Foster, and Amelia rode behind him.

After about a thousand yards, Goodluck dismounted. He knelt and inspected the ground. "He removed the moccasins and then rode northeast."

"Why would he do that?" Foster said.

"How do you know he removed the moccasins?" Adcock said.

"Beside the horse prints is a bare footprint," Goodluck said. "He mounted the saddle barefoot."

"What's to the northeast?" Goodluck said.

"The Laramie Mountains," Foster said.

"Why would he go there?" Charles said.

"I didn't say he went there," Goodluck said. "But he did go northeast, maybe to Nebraska or South Dakota, or maybe to a hideout in the mountains. One thing is for sure, we're not going to find him standing around here."

"It's too late to go now," Foster said. "Stay the night, and I'll give you a mule and all the supplies you need."

Amelia prepared a dinner consisting of soup, baked chicken, and apple pie for dessert. Water or milk was also served, with coffee afterward for the pie.

While Amelia cleared the table, Adcock, Charles, Goodluck, and Foster took their coffee and pie on the porch.

Goodluck gave each of them a Cuban cigar.

"Do you think you can track the murderer after three weeks?" Foster said.

"That's difficult to say," Goodluck said. "I will ask you this. Don't make any decisions to sell until after we return."

"How long do you plan to be gone?" Foster said.

"Ten days, two weeks, no more than that?" Goodluck said.

"The next full moon is in four nights," Foster said.

"All reports say the killer won't be back," Goodluck said. "Where are the men you have left?"

"On the ranges, including my foreman," Foster said.

"Just to be safe, have them stay in the bunkhouse," Goodluck said.

Amelia stepped out onto the porch. "I've made up the spare bedrooms," she said. "I'll show you to your rooms when you're ready."

Chapter Six

Goodluck, with the mule loaded with supplies in tow, led Charles and Adcock to the point where they'd turned around the day before.

Goodluck dismounted and inspected the tracks.

"Why do you suppose he removed the moccasins?" Charles said.

"My guess is he didn't want to wear moccasins in the mountains where you could stub a toe or step on a sharp rock," Goodluck said. "He uses the moccasins to sneak up on his victims."

"Can you track in the mountains?" Adcock said.

Goodluck mounted the saddle without answering the question and, with the mule in tow, followed the tracks.

Charles looked at Adcock.

"What?" Adcock said.

"You don't ask a man like Goodluck if he can track," Charles said.

"It was just a question," Adcock said.

"And a stupid one. Let's go."

By one in the afternoon, they were in the low foothills of the Laramie Mountains where they made camp, rested their horses and the mule, and prepared lunch.

Adcock built a fire while Charles went through the supplies and Goodluck scouted ahead.

"Mr. Foster is a generous man," Charles said. "Steaks, bacon, three dozen eggs wrapped in wax paper in a tin, cans of fruit, beans, condensed milk, sugar, coffee, and at least five pounds of cornbread."

"Well, get something cooking while I tend to the horses," Adcock said.

Goodluck returned after thirty minutes, dismounted, filled a cup with coffee, and said, "He's headed straight to the mountains and probably Nebraska."

"Well, hell, we can't track him all over the west," Adcock said.

"No, but I can visit the reservation and speak with the people," Goodluck said. "We'll track him as far as possible, and then I'll leave you and go to the reservation. Maybe somebody knows something."

"And what do we do while you're gone?"

"Go hunting, go fishing, read a book," Goodluck said. "What's for lunch?"

Goodluck read a map beside the campfire as they ate supper. "Tomorrow, I will head for the Oglala Reservation in Pine Ridge," he said.

"How long will you be gone?" Adcock said.

"A week and a bit," Goodluck said.

"While we sit on our asses?" Adcock said.

"You're not allowed on the reservation," Goodluck said. "If you want, go back to Foster and wait for me there. We can figure out what to do next when I return."

"That's what we'll do," Charles said. "Cut out enough supplies to last you the trip."

"You got enough supplies?" Charles said.

"More than enough," Goodluck said.

"We'll see you at the Foster Ranch in a week," Adcock said.

They parted ways, Goodluck traveling north, Adcock and Charles traveling south.

As they ate supper, Adcock looked at the millions of stars overhead. "I feel lost out here," he said.

"Well, we ain't lost," Charles said. "In two nights we'll be at the Foster Ranch waiting for Goodluck."

"Do you think Goodluck will find anything out about this renegade?" Adcock said.

"It's possible," Charles said. "He is one of them. If they know anything, they're more likely to tell him than a white man."

"Want some more stew?" Adcock said.

Charles held out his plate and Adcock ladled some onto it.

"We need to wire Mr. Porter when we get to Foster's," Charles said. "Laramie isn't that far from his ranch."

"And tell him what?" Adcock said.

"Good point," Charles said. "We'll wire him when Goodluck returns with some news."

Goodluck studied the stars as he rested against his saddle and ate supper. He wondered if scientists like Jules Verne took inspiration from the stars for the adventure novels they wrote.

He didn't like the fact that the renegade, if he actually was one, removed his moccasins before mounting his horse. An Indian worried about sore feet would never be a true renegade.

Could a white man so adapt as to fool other whites into believing he was an Indian?

That was very doubtful.

There were cases of kidnapped white children raised by whatever tribe captured them. The white children were taught the tribe's ways and eventually became members of the tribe, but they were never true Indians.

They could never partake in the true Sun Dance or become tribal leaders. White woman became breeders, white men became expendable in battle.

But those days were long over.

So, was this renegade the real thing, or someone who just enjoyed scalping and killing white people?

Goodluck didn't believe he was the real thing.

The moccasins convinced him of that.

After he ate and cleaned the dirty crockery, Goodluck smoked a Cuban cigar and continued to watch the stars.

"Where are you going?" Charles said.

"Relieve myself," Adcock said. "All those beans."

"Do it downwind," Charles said.

"Yeah, yeah," Adcock said.

While Charles stayed in his bedroll, Adcock walked about a hundred feet from camp to relieve himself.

The moon was full and he could see well enough to find a decent spot between some rocks to squat down. When he was finished and stood up to buckle his belt, out of the corner of his left eye he caught a glimpse of something, turned, and was struck on the forehead with tremendous force by a tomahawk.

Adcock was paralyzed, but still alive when his scalp was taken. He died in agony when the tomahawk smashed down on his neck.

In his bedroll, Charles sat up and listened carefully to the night. "Adcock, what's taking you so long?" he said.

When Adcock didn't respond, Charles stood up and removed his sidearm from the holster. "Tom? Tom, where are you? What's taking you so long?"

Scanning the shadows, using his night vision, Charles moved away from the campfire so he could see better away from the light of the flames.

"Goddammit, Tom, answer me," Charles said.

The question was answered with a tomahawk to the left side of Charles's skull that knocked him to the ground, unconscious. His scalp was removed, then Charles was left alive and conscious to die slowly and very painfully, wishing for death.

Chapter Seven

Goodluck took the south road into the Pine Ridge reservation in South Dakota. He knew warriors were posted to keep watch and, although he couldn't see them, he knew they monitored his every move.

The ride to the center of the massive reservation took half the day. He passed streams, rivers, mountains, grazing bison, grazing cattle, and fields of corn before he arrived at a settlement of cabins.

Dozens of Lakota and Oglala Sioux gathered to greet him in the town square.

"I am Joseph Goodluck of the Comanche people," Goodluck said in Lakota. "I seek the wisdom of the elders."

Goodluck sat at the table of Chief Long Wolf, who was a warrior at the Battle of the Little Bighorn and the Great Sioux Wars.

Long Wolf was a handsome man of Goodluck's age. With him at the table were several of his advisors.

Goodluck gave Long Wolf a Cuban cigar, and they smoked them with cups of strong coffee.

"I am here to seek your help with a bad situation that is happening in the Wyoming Territory," Goodluck said.

"The Ghost Warrior," Long Wolf said.

"Is that what you call him?" Goodluck said.

"I have heard the reports of a giant warrior who scalps the

whites all across Wyoming Territory," Long Wolf said. "I have spoken with the army and sent them scouts. I have spoken with the law keepers and police. My own scouts can tell me nothing of this ghost you seek. All I can tell you is, he is not of the Lakota People."

"They say he is a giant," Goodluck said.

"I have heard," Long Wolf said. "If he was one of us, I would know, and I would tell you. The reservation is all we have now, but it is ours. I have traveled east and our reservation is larger than the Rhode Island and Delaware combined. We want nothing to take this away from us."

Goodluck nodded. "Where did you travel back east?" he said.

"Washington, New York, and Boston," Long Wolf said. "I met the man they call Buffalo Bill. I am to travel with him after the snow to the place they call Europe to act in his Wild West show."

"I will tell the government that your people have nothing to do with this Ghost Warrior," Goodluck said.

"I will have a cabin prepared for you," Long Wolf said. "We will feast tonight. Tomorrow you tell the government what I told you."

Although he wasn't hungry in the morning after the feast from the night before, Goodluck didn't want to insult Long Wolf, so he ate breakfast with him in his cabin.

A hundred or more turned out to see Goodluck off as he left the reservation after breakfast.

He left Long Wolf a parting gift of six Cuban cigars.

Anxious to return to the Foster Ranch, Goodluck pushed hard. He traveled thirty miles before lunch and another thirty before dark.

He tended to his horse before he tended to himself, fed him

well, and thoroughly brushed him so that his coat was clean and dry.

Supper was beef stew and bread with coffee and condensed milk.

Goodluck watched the stars come out as he ate.

Afterward, he sipped coffee, smoked a cigar, and watched the moon rise. By the time it peaked, it was full, bright, and high in the night sky.

Goodluck felt a wave of doom pass through him. He realized his mistake in that the renegade had probably lured him north and then backtracked and headed south.

To scalp and kill again.

During the next thirty hours, Goodluck covered eighty hard miles. With each passing mile, he felt the doom in his chest grow worse.

As he rode through the foothills, Goodluck spotted buzzards circling in the sky about a mile in the distance.

He raced to the site where the buzzards circled, jumped from the saddle, and pulled his Colt revolver.

He found their camp. A dozen buzzards were picking the flesh from Charles.

Goodluck fired a shot to scatter the buzzards and stood over the body. Charles had been scalped and died from a broken neck. The first thing the buzzards had done was peck out the eyes and eat the soft flesh of the eyeballs.

Goodluck found Adcock a hundred feet away in some rocks where he'd gone to relieve himself. As with Charles, he was scalped and also had a broken neck. His eyes were eaten, as well.

Both men had been dead close to three days. The buzzards had been feasting on their flesh the entire time.

Goodluck dug two graves, removed all the men's valuables,

including the expense money, and buried them side by side. He made a Christian cross out of wood for each grave and then, wanting to return to the Foster Ranch as quickly as possible, he rode another twenty miles before dark.

Foster and his daughter were just sitting down to lunch when Goodluck arrived at their home.

"You look exhausted," Foster said.

"My horse is played out," Goodluck said. "I rode him hard."

"Amelia, ask Mr. Banks to see to Mr. Goodluck's horse," Foster said.

After Amelia left the house, Goodluck told Foster what had happened to Charles and Adcock.

"That makes up my mind," Foster said. "Tomorrow I'll go to Laramie and send a wire to Arizona and see if the man there still wants to buy my ranch. Wyoming is too uncivilized for my daughter to live in."

After lunch, Goodluck took a nap and didn't rise until dinner.

After dinner, Goodluck and Foster took coffee on the porch and watched the full moon rise in the sky.

"He isn't killing to rob them," Goodluck said.

"Sport?" Foster said.

"Tomorrow, I will go with you to Laramie to send a telegram to Mr. Porter," Goodluck. "He won't take the news well, I'm afraid."

CHAPTER EIGHT

After Porter read Goodluck's telegram, he didn't bother with the cone, but rushed to Miss Potts's office.

"Miss Potts, send emergency telegrams to Duffy and Cavill. Tell them to report immediately for an emergency," he said.

"Emergency?" Miss Potts said.

Porter gently lowered Goodluck's telegram on her desk. She read it without picking it up.

She nodded as her eyes misted up. "Right away, Mr. Porter," she said.

Goodluck shook hands with Ben Foster on the front porch.

"I wish you good luck, sir," Goodluck said. He looked at Amelia. "To you both."

Goodluck mounted his horse and began the hundred-mile journey south to Cheyenne. His horse, exhausted by the hard pace Goodluck had required on his return from the reservation, had recovered. Still, Goodluck didn't want to push him again so soon, so he kept the pace to thirty miles a day.

In a week's time, when he returned to the office, maybe he could deal with his own shame before he had to face Mr. Porter.

The slower pace gave Goodluck time to reflect. At the time, traveling to the reservation to try to obtain information seemed like a better course of action than trying to track someone through the mountains for weeks on end.

He didn't see any signs that the renegade had backtracked,

but in the mountains it would have been impossible to spot them anyway.

Maybe he should have had Adcock and Charles ride with him to the reservation, camp outside, and wait for him. Then, it seemed a waste of time to have them go with him, when they could have returned to the Foster Ranch and picked up possible fresh news.

While he wasn't close to Adcock and Charles, they were good men, devoted to their jobs and Mr. Porter. For them to die the way they did left a scar on Goodluck's heart.

A scar that could only be healed by finding this renegade and bringing him to justice.

Porter was too sick to his stomach to eat lunch. He took a Cuban cigar to the small park across the street from the office and sat on a bench to smoke it.

He hadn't lost a man in the line of duty in a decade. It was a bitter pill to swallow, knowing that he'd sent two men to their deaths. It was the primary reason for the "no married men" rule he strictly enforced.

Losing a man was difficult enough. Having to break the news to a man's wife and children was more than he could bear.

As he smoked the cigar, Miss Potts entered the park and sat beside him.

"I sent the telegrams to Mr. Duffy and Mr. Cavill," she said.

Porter nodded. "Miss Potts, it is days like this when I ponder retirement," he said.

"Nonsense, sir," Miss Potts said. "I have worked for you for ten years, and I am always astonished at how you always fail to realize how important the work you do is. Hundreds of criminals and outlaws have been brought to justice because of you. Presidents are alive because of you. New and modern methods of preventing crime are being used across the country because of the work you do. Retirement? You wouldn't last one day at home with nothing to do."

"Miss Potts, every day I thank God for you," Porter said. "Let's go back to work."

"Yes sir," Miss Potts said.

Chapter Nine

James Duffy and Sylvia Trent rode along the south range of her father's ranch, which was located ten miles west of Miles City in Montana.

They dismounted at a clearing beside a creek running through the property.

"This area here was designated by my father as where we will build our home when we marry," Sylvia said. "From this spot, it is only twelve miles to Miles City, if you decide to open a law practice once you finish attending law school."

Duffy had to admit it was a beautiful place to build a home. And Sylvia was the most beautiful woman he had ever met. Tall and slender, she had green eyes, dark hair, and flawless skin.

They met when he was on assignment in Montana not long ago. He and his partner, Jack Cavill, were assigned to catch cattle thieves. The case proved much more difficult than anticipated.

"What do you think?" Sylvia said.

"It certainly is a perfect spot for a home, no doubt," Duffy said.

"Father understands you would rather practice law in town than work as a ranch hand," Sylvia said. "And Miles City could certainly use an attorney."

Duffy looked at the lush green area where the house would be built. "Your father is a generous man," he said.

"My father doesn't want to lose me," Sylvia said. "He knows

I will go wherever you go, so what better way to keep me close than to build us a home?"

Duffy felt nervous as he reached into the right pocket of his suit jacket and removed the ring box. After his last assignment, he took a trip to Chicago to shop for the ring in the large jewelry stores. He'd found what he thought was the perfect ring with which to propose marriage to Sylvia.

He'd found a one-and-a-half karat, emerald-cut diamond set in a beautiful, six-prong gold ring. He estimated Sylvia's ring size at six. The stone and band cost a bit over a thousand dollars.

Usually well-spoken, Duffy often found himself at a loss for words around Sylvia, so he didn't try an elaborate proposal. He opened the box and offered it to her. She looked at the ring and nodded yes.

He slipped the ring on Sylvia's finger. She looked at it and then hugged him tight around the waist.

"I promise you I will give you many fine children," she said.

"I still have some things I need to work out," Duffy said. "Where I should finish law school, how do I manage Jack's fighting career, and what do I tell Mr. Porter?"

"You only have one year of law school left," Sylvia said. "Finish it in Chicago while I see to our house being built. Jack Cavill is a very big boy and can manage his own affairs, and Mr. Porter will just have to get along without you."

Duffy looked at Sylvia.

"James, I feel like being naughty in the physical sense," Sylvia said.

"Your father wouldn't approve," Duffy said.

"My father isn't here," Sylvia said.

"Before I weaken, we'd best get back," Duffy said.

"All right, James," Sylvia said.

They rode back to the ranch where Douglas Trent, Sylvia's

father, waited in a chair on the porch. He held a mug of coffee and smoked a cigar.

At the hitching post, Sylvia rushed from the saddle to the porch to show Trent her new ring.

"Father, look," she said.

"It's beautiful, sweetheart," Trent said. He shook Duffy's hand as Duffy stepped onto the porch. "James, this came for you," he said and handed Duffy the telegram.

Duffy looked at the Western Union envelope. "It's from Mr. Porter," he said.

"Come in the house with me, Sylvia, so I can get my glasses and see your ring," Trent said.

In the morning, dressed in black trail clothes, his .44 Smith & Wesson revolver on his hip, Duffy said goodbye to Sylvia and Trent on the porch.

"I don't understand why you have to be at his beck and calling all the time," Sylvia said.

"It's an emergency," Duffy said. "I wouldn't go otherwise."

"Well, go on and go then. See if I care," Sylvia snapped.

"I'll wire you from Springfield," Duffy said.

"Just go," Sylvia said.

Duffy nodded to Trent, mounted his horse, and started for the road to Miles City.

"Sylvia, sit down," Trent said.

"Why, Father?"

"Just sit down," Trent said.

Sylvia took a chair. Trent stood.

"You are a truly beautiful young woman, of that there is no denying, but you are spoiled rotten," Trent said.

"Father," Sylvia said.

"The sin of it is that it is not your fault, but mine," Trent said. "After your mother died, I lavished everything on you and spoiled you terribly."

"How can you say such things to me?" Sylvia said.

"Because they are true," Trent said. "James is as fine a man as I have ever known, and he is a man of honor. The fact that you don't understand why he is leaving tells me you are a woman in body but a child in mind. You think on that. Hard."

Trent turned and entered the house, leaving Sylvia alone with her thoughts, which quickly turned to the ring on her finger. She admired it in the sunlight.

Chapter Ten

Jack Cavill worked out on the heavy bag in the barn at Joey Jordan's ranch outside of Helena in Montana. The bag wasn't a professional one from a store, but a large canvas sack made from hemp and filled with one hundred twenty pounds of grain, stitched together and hung from a chain from a rafter.

As he pounded the bag, Joey Jordan leaned over a stall fence and watched.

Joey was short for Josephine and she was the prettiest girl Cavill ever laid eyes upon. Twenty-eight years old, with deep red hair and hazel colored eyes, she was a sight to behold.

After her father died, she took control of his ranch and worked as hard as any of the hands. It was but a handful of times Jack had seen her wear a skirt, as she mostly wore trail clothes like the men.

And she wasn't ashamed to show the calluses on her hands the way some women were.

Standing six-foot-four inches tall, weighing two hundred and fifty pounds, Cavill was the largest, most powerful man Joey had ever seen. At first, the things he would do would astonish her, but as she grew more and more accustomed to his ways, she realized that deep down, he was like a little boy in many ways.

He spent three days fighting with a large stump when he could have hitched a team of mules and let them do the work, but he insisted on wasting those days digging and shoving and ripping the damn thing from the earth.

It puzzled her why a grown man would do such a foolish thing until she realized that, to Jack, it was a challenge, and the one thing he never backed down from was a challenge.

A few days ago they took the wagon to Helena for some fencing supplies. After the wagon was loaded, she went to the general store for a few personal items and Cavill went to the tobacco shop for some cigars.

Returning to the wagon with her arms full of packages, Joey was accosted by three cowboys who'd had a bit too much whiskey at the saloon. There were many other men on the streets, but they did nothing to help Joey as the three cowboys pried at the packages and tried to kiss her.

All of a sudden, Cavill was there. He picked up one cowboy as if he was a doll and flung him into the street. Then he grabbed the other two, smashed their heads together, and tossed them onto the wood sidewalk.

"You boys need to learn your manners," Cavill said as he helped her into the wagon as if nothing had happened.

Then Joey realized that, to Jack Cavill, nothing *had* happened.

"How long are you going to beat on that silly thing?" Joey said.

"I'm fighting Charlie Mitchell in two weeks, honey. I have to be ready," Cavill said.

"We need to go to town," Joey said.

"What for?" Cavill said.

"I suppose I can go alone," Joey said.

Cavill paused. "Give me a few minutes to wash up and change," he said.

While in town, Joey stopped by the post office for the mail and the telegraph office to check for telegrams from the auction houses, of which there were several. There was also a telegram for Cavill from his employer, Charles Porter.

She knew the telegram was bad news, that Porter needed Cavill for some reason or another. She knew, if he read the telegram, he would pack up and go because of his sense of duty.

As she walked to the wagon, Joey hid the telegram from Porter in her handbag.

Cavill had already loaded up the fencing supplies and was waiting for her. "Need anything else?" he said.

"No, let's get this stuff home," Joey said.

As he drove the wagon, Joey grew silent as she wrestled with her conscience. Finally, halfway home, she said, "Stop the wagon."

"What?" Cavill said.

"Stop the wagon," Joey said.

Cavill slowed the wagon to a stop.

"Is something wrong?" Cavill said.

Joey sighed as she dug the telegram out of her handbag and handed it to Cavill. He opened the envelope and read the contents.

"How bad is it?" Joey said.

Cavill handed her the telegram to read.

"You have to go, don't you?" Joey said.

"For just a little while," Cavill said.

Cavill woke up during the night when Joey started crying next to him in bed. He struck a match, lit the lamp on the nightstand, and sat up in the bed.

"What is it, honey?" he said.

"I've never loved a man before, Jack," Joey said. "I don't want to lose you, not now, not ever."

"I have to go," Cavill said.

"I know," Joey said. "And I'm sorry I tried to deceive you. I just love you so much, is all. Forgive me?"

"There's nothing to forgive," Cavill said. "Look, I'll be gone a few weeks, and then I'll be back. Don't worry."

"What if you get killed?" Joey said.

"I'm not so easy to kill, honey," Cavill said. "Don't you worry about that."

In the morning, Joey sat on the porch and cried as Cavill mounted his horse and rode away.

Chapter Eleven

Duffy reported to the office first and was given a complete report by Goodluck and Porter.

"Adcock and Charles were good men," Duffy said.

"Yes they were," Porter said.

"What do you want us to do?" Duffy said.

Porter picked up his cone. "Miss Potts, when is Mr. Cavill due?"

"His telegram said day after tomorrow," Miss Potts replied.

"Ask me that in two days' time," Porter said.

Duffy and Goodluck went to lunch at a small restaurant a block from the office.

"Whoever he is, he out-tracked me and out-thought me," Goodluck said. "I would have thought it impossible to be fooled when tracking a man, but he did just that."

"You were tracking a man into the mountains who had a two-week head start," Duffy said. "All he had to do was sit and wait."

"Maybe so, but I was fooled and it cost us two good men," Goodluck said.

"You don't know that," Duffy said. "He could have simply stumbled upon them and taken advantage of the opportunity. And besides, if you had stayed behind with them, who is to say we wouldn't have lost three good men."

Goodluck looked at Duffy. "I want this bastard, James," he

said. "I want to track him and find him and hang him from a tree."

"As soon as Jack gets here, you just might get the chance," Duffy said.

For the next two days, Duffy read all the reports several times and made pages of notes. He went to dinner with Porter and Goodluck, and they discussed the case over steaks.

"There must be some logical reason why he chooses the full moon to murder his victims," Porter said.

"I've studied all the reports and have thought about that," Duffy said. "It's not unlike the legend of the werewolf in England on the moors."

"Yes, but that's fantasy," Porter said.

"But no less frightening," Duffy said. "Right now he has an entire territory on edge, waiting for the next full moon, wondering where he's going to strike next, and asking themselves, 'Will it be me?' It's terrifying to live that way and I think that's what he wants. To terrify the people in Wyoming."

"The question is why? What does he gain? Even a madman needs a reason to act," Porter said.

"We won't know his reason until we catch him," Duffy said.

"The next full moon is in ten days," Porter said. "That's not enough time to get to Wyoming and track him down before he strikes again. He could be anywhere in the territory in ten days."

"Jack will be here tomorrow," Duffy said. "We'll leave as soon as he gets here."

Porter looked at Goodluck. "And you?"

"Wild horses couldn't keep me from going," Goodluck said.

Porter nodded. "I'll wire Governor Hale in the morning," he said.

Cavill arrived at the office shortly after nine in the morning.

Miss Potts gave him a cup of coffee on his way into Porter's office.

Porter, Duffy, and Goodluck were seated around the conference table scanning stacks of documents.

"Have a seat, Mr. Cavill," Porter said. "We were just discussing when you should leave."

"I just got here," Cavill said.

"Mr. Cavill, this issue has become very personal to me," Porter said. "Two men in my employ have been murdered in the line of duty. I expect the man responsible—white, red, or black—to be brought to justice. I don't want him shot, I don't want him hung. I want him arrested for trial."

Porter stood and went to his desk and picked up the cone. "Miss Potts?" he said.

A few seconds later, the door opened and she entered.

"Get three tickets to Cheyenne on the noon train," Porter said.

"Right away," Miss Potts said.

Porter returned to the conference table. "Mr. Cavill, pack your gear, draw your horse from the stable, and meet Mr. Duffy and Mr. Goodluck at the station at eleven-thirty. They will give you full reports on the ride. I shall be there to see you off."

"Can I finish my coffee first?" Cavill said.

Cavill went to the apartment he kept near the office, changed clothes, and packed his gear. He made sure he had plenty of ammunition for his Colt revolver and Winchester rifle.

Then he walked to the stables and met Duffy and Goodluck.

Cavill walked Blue, his very tall horse, out of the stables, followed by Duffy, who rode a smaller, faster horse named Bull.

Goodluck followed with his own horse.

Together they rode to the railroad depot and met Mr. Porter.

"Governor Hale is expecting you," Porter said. He handed

Duffy an envelope. "Twenty thousand for expenses. Wire me when you arrive in Cheyenne."

"We will," Duffy said.

"And Mr. Cavill, I want him alive," Porter said.

Chapter Twelve

"Why does Mr. Porter always assume I'm going to kill somebody?" Cavill said.

"Are you serious, Jack?" Duffy said.

Goodluck grinned, then picked up his coffee cup and took a sip.

They were in the dining car at a table beside the window. For the better part of an hour, Goodluck told Duffy and Cavill about what had transpired in Wyoming and during his visit to the reservation.

"Well, maybe I fly off the handle once in a while," Cavill said.

"Once in a while?" Duffy said.

The waiter arrived with lunch: baked chicken with potatoes and carrots.

"Any idea why the full moon?" Cavill said as he cut into his chicken.

"Fear," Duffy said. "Everybody in Wyoming Territory is on edge, waiting for the next full moon. He's got everybody terrified they'll be next."

"Like that werewolf story in England," Cavill said.

"I didn't think you read, Jack," Duffy said.

"Maybe I don't read law books, but I've read a book or two," Cavill said.

"How does the werewolf story go?" Goodluck said. "I haven't read it."

"Every month, under a full moon, a person who is cursed

changes into a wolf and kills someone," Duffy said. "If someone is bitten by this wolf and survives, then they also are cursed and become a wolf under a full moon."

"I think it's a pretty lazy way to terrorize people," Cavill said.

"What?" Duffy said.

"Think about it," Cavill said. "He's got an entire territory scared to death, and he only has to kill once a month to keep them on edge the other twenty-nine days."

Duffy and Goodluck looked at each other.

"Makes sense in a Jack kind of way," Duffy said.

"Sure," Cavill said.

"But let me ask you this, Jack," Duffy said. "What does he gain?"

"How the hell do I know," Cavill said. "I'll beat it out of him when we catch him."

Goodluck grinned.

"And you wonder why Mr. Porter always assumes you're going to kill someone," Duffy said.

After lunch, they went to the gentlemen's car. Duffy, Cavill, and Goodluck smoked Cuban cigars over a small glass of brandy.

"He's a big man, judging from his footprint," Goodluck said. "Maybe not as big as Jack, but large. The witnesses are correct in that he is not white, but an Indian. He tracks, rides, and kills like an Indian. More important, he thinks like an Indian, or the Indians of the past."

"How does an Indian think?" Cavill said.

"Much different than you," Goodluck said.

"How so?" Cavill said.

"If you have a problem with someone, what do you do?" Goodluck said.

"Confront him," Cavill said.

"Jim would try to reason first and you would raise a fist,"

Goodluck said. "But the Indian would wait for the right time to solve his problem. Even if it meant weeks, months, or years, he would wait. My people are far more patient than yours."

"That still doesn't explain this full moon business," Cavill said. "Or his reason for killing and scalping people in the first place."

"No, it doesn't," Goodluck said. "A true renegade wouldn't use the cycle of the moon to strike fear into his enemies. He would let his actions do it for him. The man we're after has a purpose to his method."

"And when we find him, I'll beat it out of him," Cavill said.

Duffy and Goodluck grinned.

"In the meantime, we have to find him," Duffy said.

Duffy had marked all the sites of the murders on a map of Wyoming Territory. The three detectives studied the map over dinner.

"There doesn't seem to be any real pattern to how he selects his victims other than wherever he happens to be at the full moon is where he strikes," Duffy said.

"When I set out to track him, he had a two-week head start," Goodluck said. "That he was able to pick up on us, backtrack, and kill Charles and Adcock means he was close. Maybe he has a place in the mountains, or maybe it was just coincidence. My guess is we won't know where he is until he strikes again."

"When is the next full moon?" Cavill said.

"Eight nights from now," Duffy said.

"Wyoming is a big territory," Cavill said. "He could be anywhere."

Duffy looked at the map. "This is one man I'll enjoy watching hang," he said.

Shortly after breakfast, the train arrived in Cheyenne.

Duffy, Cavill, and Goodluck retrieved their horses and walked through town to the office of Governor Hale.

"This used to be the wildest town short of Deadwood," Cavill said. "Look at it now. Schools, churches, fancy restaurants. I bet there isn't a decent saloon left from the old days."

"We're not here for saloons," Duffy said.

"Must be four thousand people living here now," Cavill said.

"It's a railroad hub," Duffy said. "Let's go see the governor."

Chapter Thirteen

Governor Hale met Duffy, Cavill, and Goodluck in his office. He had an aide bring coffee to the conference table.

"Two ranchers and one farmer have sold out and moved away," Hale said. "One of the ranchers was Ben Foster. We can ill afford to lose a man like Foster. Wyoming needs to grow if we're to become a state, and right now we're going backwards, losing the very citizens we need to accomplish our goal."

"Governor, we're here to help, but we need your help in return," Duffy said.

"Anything I can do, just ask," Hale said.

"You're appointed by the president," Duffy said. "That gives you federal powers elected governors don't have. The railroad is federal and inside Wyoming Territory under your command. I would like you to secure a train for us and keep it ready to travel at a moment's notice. If he kills again, I want to be able to be at the site within twelve hours or less anywhere in Wyoming Territory."

Hale nodded. "I'll arrange it," he said.

"One riding car and boxcar for our horses will do," Duffy said.

"That shouldn't be a problem," Hale said. "What else?"

"Send an executive order to every marshal, county sheriff, and sheriff that if anybody is scalped and murdered in their town or jurisdiction, they are not to disturb the bodies until we arrive. You have seven days to notify everyone of this order."

"Let me see if I understand this," Hale said. "If he strikes again, you want the victim or victims to stay as they lay until you arrive, is that correct?"

"That's correct, Governor," Duffy said. "We can learn a great deal from a crime scene if it's undisturbed."

"Charles told me you men are experts in what they call forensics," Hale said. "I'll see to your requests right away."

"Thank you, Governor," Duffy said. "We'll be at the Cheyenne Hotel."

As they walked their horses to the Cheyenne Hotel, Duffy, Cavill, and Goodluck drew stares from people on the street. The lawless days of Cheyenne were well behind it, and seeing men armed with sidearms and rifles seemed almost out of place.

"What is it with these people?" Cavill said. "They're looking at us like we forgot to put our pants on."

"I guess they've never seen so fine a male specimen as you walking down their streets, Jack," Duffy said.

"I got half a mind to—" Cavill said.

"Here's the hotel," Goodluck said.

They tied the horses to the hitching post and entered the lobby.

"James Duffy, Jack Cavill, and Joseph Goodluck," Duffy said to the desk clerk. "We have reservations made by our employer, Charles Porter."

The clerk scanned his logbook. "Three rooms on the third floor," he said.

"We'll be back after we stable our horses," Duffy said.

After a shave, a bath, and putting on clean clothes, Cavill went down to the lobby. There he found Duffy seated in a chair with a cup of coffee and writing paper.

"Writing Sylvia?" Cavill said.

"She was madder than a plucked chicken when I left," Duffy said.

"Where's Goodluck?" Cavill said.

"The blacksmith's," Duffy said. "He's having extra shoes made for our horses in case we do some hard riding."

"Joey wasn't mad, but she cried like a schoolgirl when I left," Cavill said.

"All women react differently," Duffy said. "Why not write a letter to Joey?"

"And say what?"

"How you feel."

"How I feel is pissed-off mad at having to miss fighting Charlie Mitchell, is how I feel," Cavill said.

"No, about how you feel about her," Duffy said.

"She knows."

"Write a few words and let her know you're alive and you miss her," Duffy said and handed Cavill a sheet of paper and a pencil.

"I never know what to write," Cavill said.

"She'll be happy just to hear from you."

"Yeah?"

"Yeah."

Cavill took a seat and started to write.

After a few minutes, Duffy said, "Let me see what you wrote."

Cavill showed him the paper. *"Hello, it's Jack,"* Duffy said. "For God's sake, Jack, tear this up."

"You said she'd be happy . . ." Cavill said.

"Never mind what I said, start over," Duffy said, and he gave Cavill another sheet of paper. "And start with *My Dear Joey.*"

"Eighteen shoes. That will be nine dollars," the blacksmith said.

Goodluck opened his wallet and removed a ten dollar bill. "Give me a dollar's work of nails for the shoes."

"What about tools?"

"I got those. Thanks."

Goodluck carried the shoes and nails to the stables connected to the hotel and put them in his saddlebags in his horse's stall. Then he took the time to brush and groom his horse and gave him a few sugar cubes to satisfy his sweet tooth.

He met Duffy and Cavill in front of the hotel.

"We mailed a few letters, and I sent a wire to Porter with our plans," Duffy said.

"When are we going to get some dinner?" Cavill said. "We missed lunch, and I'm starved."

"Let's try the hotel dining room," Duffy said.

They went into the dining room, got a window table, and ordered steaks.

"I'm going to go stir-crazy sitting around this town the next seven days waiting for him to strike again," Cavill said.

"We'll find something to do tomorrow," Duffy said.

"Like what?" Cavill said.

Chapter Fourteen

After breakfast the following morning, Duffy, Cavill, and Goodluck took coffee on the porch of the hotel.

"It's a fine morning," Duffy said.

"I'm going *loco,*" Cavill said. "I need something to do."

"We are doing something. We're waiting," Duffy said.

"Something a bit more stimulating," Cavill said. "This kind of waiting is giving me splinters."

"Jack, we made a plan, and we're sticking to it," Duffy said.

A deputy sheriff approached the hotel and paused at the steps to the porch. "Are you the detectives from back east?" he said.

"Back east?" Cavill said. "You consider Illinois the east?"

"East of Colorado is back east to me," the deputy said.

Cavill dug his cigar case out of his left boot and lit a cigar with a wood match. "That's fascinating, Deputy, but is there something you want?" he said.

"No," the deputy said. "But the sheriff does."

"And what does the sheriff want?" Cavill said.

"He didn't tell me. He just said it was important," the deputy said.

Duffy stood up. "Let's go see what the sheriff wants," he said.

"I'm Sheriff Devens. Thanks for coming over," Devens said. "Why don't you boys have a seat?"

Duffy, Cavill, and Goodluck took chairs in the sheriff's office opposite the desk where Devens sat.

"Deputy, get some coffee for these men," Devens said.

The deputy went to the woodstove in the corner of the office and filled three cups with coffee from the pot.

"What did you want to see us about, Sheriff?" Duffy said.

"I received word from the governor about you men," Devens said. "So I thought I'd get your take on a situation I have here."

"And what situation is that?" Duffy said as he took a cup from the deputy.

"I have a prisoner in back named Joe Gordon," Devens said. "He's twenty-four, has a young wife and baby, and has a small spread north of town. He got into a card game at the Occidental Hotel and lost badly to a card cheat named McFee. The next night, McFee was found murdered and robbed in an alleyway."

"Did he do it?" Duffy said.

"I've known this boy since he was ten years old," Devens said.

"That wasn't my question," Duffy said.

"A jury found him guilty," Devens said. "I'm to take him to Leavenworth next week, where he is to serve a twenty-year sentence."

"And you don't think he's guilty?" Duffy said.

"I have my doubts," Devens said.

"And why is that?" Duffy said.

"I've never known Joe Gordon to commit a violent act in his life," Devens said. "The night he lost at cards, he wasn't carrying a gun. In fact, I've never even seen him wear one."

"You said the card shark was murdered the following night," Cavill said. "Was Gordon in town that night?"

"He says he wasn't," Devens said. "No one saw him, but who is to say he didn't slip in and out unseen?"

"How much did he lose?" Cavill said.

"Ten dollars," Devens said.

"Ten dollars?" Duffy said. "He killed a man for ten dollars?"

"That's how the jury saw it," Devens said.

"How do you see it?" Duffy said.

"I don't know. I just don't know," Devens said.

"How did you come to arrest him if no one saw him in town?" Duffy said.

"Let me take a step back," Devens said. "Gordon is not usually a gambling man, but as he said in court, he had ten dollars burning a hole in his pocket that night and decided to try his luck. He started out with ten dollars and hit a lucky streak and was up to three hundred when the card shark, a fellow named McFee, sat down. Inside of an hour, Gordon lost it all, including his ten dollars. They had words. Gordon called him a cheat before he left the saloon."

"And is he?" Cavill said.

"I checked as best I could," Devens said. "His reputation is that he's good, but has never been caught cheating."

"Was he married?" Duffy said.

"His widow stayed in town to watch me take Gordon to the train next week," Devens said.

"Other than the fact that Gordon called him a cheat, what other proof is there?" Duffy said.

"Here is where it gets tricky," Devens said. "McFee and his wife were returning from a late supper and took a shortcut through the alley between the general store and the freight office. She said a man blocked their path and aimed a gun at McFee and shot him twice in the chest and then ran off. She only saw this man for a second, but she identified Gordon in court as the shooter."

"Did she know Gordon before the shooting?" Duffy said.

"Claims she never saw him before," Devens said.

"Then how did you come to arrest him?" Cavill said.

"My jurisdiction ends at the town line," Devens said. "I requested the US Marshal to take charge, and we went to see everybody who sat in on the card game where Gordon lost to McFee. We found six hundred dollars hidden in an old coffee can at Gordon's house, and the revolver he keeps in the house had been recently fired. We arrested him on suspicion, and Mrs. McFee identified Gordon as the man who killed her husband. She also said her husband won six hundred the night before."

"So why the doubts then?" Cavill said.

"Gordon claims the six hundred is his life's savings and he fired his gun at some snakes recently when he was planting," Devens said. "He skinned them for meat. We found two snakes hanging in the root cellar."

"He's in back?" Duffy said.

Devens nodded.

"Can we see him?" Cavill said.

"I was hoping you'd say that," Devens said.

Devens stood from his desk, grabbed a key, and walked to the door leading to the holding cells.

Gordon was the only prisoner. He was a tall, thin man with finely cut features, sandy hair, and liquid brown eyes.

"Stand up, Joe," Devens said. "These men want to talk to you."

Gordon stood up.

"My name is James Duffy. The big fellow is Jack Cavill, and the other is Joseph Goodluck," Duffy said. "We are detectives from the Illinois Detective Agency and also federally appointed constables authorized to enforce the law in all states and territories. Do you understand what I just said?"

"Yes, sir," Gordon said.

"Sheriff, open the cell, please," Duffy said.

Devens unlocked the door. Duffy, Cavill, Goodluck, and Devens entered.

"Have a seat, son," Duffy said.

Gordon sat on the bunk.

"Goodluck, get the chair in the hallway," Duffy said.

Goodluck grabbed the chair from the hallway.

"Jack, you want to do the honors?" Duffy said.

Cavill moved the chair opposite Gordon and sat.

"Put your hands on your legs, palms up," Cavill said. "Don't worry. I'm not going to hurt you."

Gordon placed his hands on his legs, palms up. Cavill felt the pulse on Gordon's wrists.

"What's your name?" Duffy said.

"Joseph Thaddeus Gordon," Gordon said.

"Your age?" Duffy said.

"Twenty-four."

"Are you married?"

"Yes."

"Children?"

"A baby girl."

"Did you recently lose at a card game?"

"Yes."

"Do you think the man who beat you cheated?"

"I do, but I have no proof."

"Did you kill the gambler named McFee?"

"Of course not."

"The six hundred dollars in a coffee can at your home, where did you get it?"

"My wife and I saved it," Gordon said. "When my pa died, he left us two hundred. We farm the land he left us. Our usual crop brings us three hundred a year. I earn extra money busting horses, and my wife takes in sewing. We saved every penny we could so we could buy another forty acres of land for sale next to ours."

"Do you own a gun?" Duffy said.

"I have a Winchester 73 for hunting and a Smith and Wesson .44 for personal protection from snakes and such when I'm working the fields."

"Did you shoot and kill two snakes in the field recently?"

"The day before the card game."

Duffy looked at Cavill and Cavill nodded.

"Okay, thank you," Duffy said.

"What's this all about?" Gordon said.

"We'll get back to you," Duffy said.

Duffy, Cavill, Goodluck, and Devens returned to the office.

"I have the same question. What was that all about?" Devens said.

"Sheriff, there is no way in hell that kid killed that gambler," Cavill said.

"Why do you say so?" Devens said.

"When a man is calm, so is his pulse," Cavill said. "But when a man is under stress, his heart beats faster. This kid's heart rate never skipped a beat. There is no way he could have lied and kept a slow, steady pulse."

"I see," Devens said.

"The doctor who did the autopsy on McFee, can we talk to him?" Duffy said.

"Sure, but why?" Devens said.

"We want to do a ballistics test," Cavill said.

"A what?"

Chapter Fifteen

"Doctor Jenkins, these men are . . . oh, never mind," Devens said. "Boys, tell the doc what you want."

Jenkins, a man in his sixties, had been practicing medicine for nearly forty years. He looked at Duffy, Cavill, and Goodluck. "Yes?" he said.

"The bullets you took out of the gambler McFee, did you save them?" Duffy said.

"I save and catalogue all bullets I remove from every man, dead or alive," Jenkins said.

"We'll be back," Duffy said.

As they walked back to Devens's office, Cavill said, "Do you have Gordon's Smith and Wesson?"

"In the office," Devens said.

"A gunsmith?" Duffy said.

"A few blocks from my office," Devens said.

"Good," Duffy said.

"Swede, these boys are detectives and want to use your firing range," Devens said.

"Do you have a sandbag?" Duffy said.

"A what?" Swede said.

"A bag filled with sand," Cavill said.

"Where in the hell would I get a bag filled with sand?" Swede said.

"We'll use dirt," Cavill said.

"Dirt? Sheriff, what the hell is going on?" Swede said.

"Just do as they ask," Devens said.

Goodluck hung the forty-pound bag of dirt from a pole in the backyard shooting range of the Swede's gun shop.

Jack loaded Gordon's Smith & Wesson revolver with fresh ammunition, aimed, and fired six shots into the bag in a tight-knit group.

"That will do," Cavill said.

"What will do?" Swede said.

"Not even close," Duffy said when he compared the bullets taken from McFee's body to the bullets fired from Gordon's revolver under Doctor Jenkins's microscope.

"Mind explaining what you're looking at?" Devens said.

"Every gun, rifle and revolver, makes its own mark on a bullet," Duffy said. "No two anywhere in the world are alike. The markings on the bullets from Gordon's gun are not even close to the marking on the bullets taken from McFee's body. Look for yourself."

Devens peered through the microscope.

"What am I looking at?" Devens said.

"The bullet from Gordon's gun," Duffy said. He replaced the bullet with one from McFee's body. "See the difference?"

Devens looked up.

"His gun didn't kill McFee?" Devens said.

"No," Duffy said.

"Then who the hell did?" Devens said.

"That's up to you to find out," Cavill said.

"Boys, I don't want to take him to prison. Can you help me out?" Devens said.

Over lunch at the hotel, Duffy said, "So what do you want to do? We can't let an innocent man spend twenty years in prison, and like you said, Jack, we got six more days of sitting around doing nothing."

"Let's go see the sheriff after lunch," Cavill said.

"Do you have a list of the other men at the table the night Gordon lost to McFee?" Duffy said.

"Sure do. Why?" Devens said.

"We'd like to do a ballistics test on their guns," Cavill said.

"Two live in town," Devens said.

"We'll start with them," Duffy said.

The first of the two men who lived in town was Able Johnson, who worked at one of the stables in Cheyenne. He was shoveling manure when they went to see him.

"Mr. Johnson, I need to see you for a moment," Devens said.

"Kinda busy right now. What do you want?" Johnson said.

"Do you own a gun?" Devens said.

"Somewhere. In the desk, I think," Johnson said.

"Could you get it for me, please?" Devens said.

"What for?" Johnson said.

"Just get the gun, Able," Devens said.

Johnson walked inside the stable office, opened the desk, and returned with an old Colt revolver. He handed it to Devens, who handed it to Cavill.

Cavill cocked the hammer. "Firing pin is busted and there's enough rust inside the barrel, this thing would never fire," he said.

"Is this your only gun?" Devens said.

"I make four dollars a day shoveling shit and feeding horses. I ain't got the money for buying guns," Johnson said.

"Mr. Cassedy, can I see you for a moment?" Devens said.

Cassedy was one of two blacksmiths in Cheyenne. He stepped

out from behind a large bellows.

"I'm busy, Sheriff. What do you want?" Cassedy said.

"I need to see your sidearm," Devens said.

"What for?" Cassedy said.

"These men are detectives," Devens said. "They're helping me sort some things out."

"What's that got to do with my piece?" Cassedy said.

Cassedy was a large man and used to getting his own way.

"Just get your gun," Devens said.

"I don't believe I will," Cassedy said. "You don't have just cause to take my gun."

Cavill looked past Cassedy and saw the holster hanging on a hook on the back wall. He walked past Cassedy to the wall and removed the gun from the holster.

"Hey, you son of a bitch, what do you think you're doing?" Cassedy said.

"Borrowing your sidearm," Cavill said.

As Cavill walked past Cassedy, Cassedy swung a fist at Cavill. Cavill sidestepped the punch, spun, and punched Cassedy in the stomach.

The air left Cassedy as he slumped to his knees.

"Jim, this is a Remington .38," Cavill said as he tossed the gun onto a table.

"Sorry to have bothered you, Mr. Cassedy," Duffy said.

As they walked to the door, Cassedy stood up, grabbed a hammer, and swung it at Cavill.

Cavill caught Cassedy's wrist, bent it down and backward, and the hammer fell from Cassedy's hand.

"Bad move, Mr. Cassedy," Duffy said.

Cavill shoved Cassedy backward, turned, and walked away.

Cavill, Duffy, Goodluck, and Devens sat in chairs on the porch of the hotel with cups of coffee.

Cavill and Goodluck smoked cigars.

"Well, boys, I do appreciate all you've done so far," Devens said. "I'll have to get the marshal involved to check the other three who live out of town."

"It beats sitting on our asses the next week," Cavill said.

"Here comes the widow McFee," Devens said.

Mrs. McFee was a very attractive woman of about thirty, with blond hair worn up in a bun. She wore a bright, fashionable dress and carried a matching handbag. She paused on the porch.

"I am looking forward to watching you take that murderer to the train in five days, Sheriff," she said. "So I can take my leave of this filthy town for good."

"I'm sorry you feel that way, ma'am," Devens said.

"How am I supposed to feel after watching my husband murdered in cold blood?" Mrs. McFee said. "Goodnight."

After she entered the hotel, Devens said, "Well, boys, I best make my rounds and see what my deputies are up to."

"We'll have breakfast in the morning before we head out," Duffy said.

"Goodnight," Devens said and left the porch.

"Jack, are you thinking what I'm thinking?" Duffy said.

"If you're thinking the widow McFee is dressed a bit too gay for a woman who just lost her husband, then yeah, I'm thinking what you're thinking," Cavill said.

"Goodluck, do you think you can follow the widow McFee tomorrow and see where she goes?" Duffy said.

"I can. Why?" Goodluck said.

"Call it a hunch," Duffy said.

Chapter Sixteen

Goodluck sat in a chair in the lobby with a cup of coffee and a newspaper. He read English as well as any college graduate. His French and Spanish weren't as strong as his English, but they were still very good.

A few minutes past ten in the morning, the widow McFee appeared in the lobby. She wore her blond hair up as she had the previous night and wore a bright blue dress with a matching handbag.

She left the lobby, and Goodluck gave her a minute or so head start. With a dress like hers, she would be easy to spot.

He left the hotel, picked her up on the street, and followed her from a safe distance to the livery stable where his horse was boarded.

Goodluck found a discreet spot across the street and watched as she entered the livery office.

Minutes later, a stable hand walked a buggy from the barn to the office. The widow came out, and he helped her into the seat.

She tugged the reins and drove the buggy north.

Goodluck waited until she was out of sight, then entered the stables and saddled his horse.

He gave her a long head start. The buggy was easy to track, and he had no problem picking up the trail.

She left Cheyenne, still traveling north along the freight road.

About an hour later, still traveling a safe distance behind the buggy, the tracks suddenly turned to the left, onto a pasture of green grass.

He followed for fifty yards, dismounted, and tied his horse to a tree. He removed the field binoculars from a saddlebag and set out on foot, following the tracks in the grass made by the buggy.

Three quarters of a mile later, Goodluck paused and watched from behind a tree as the widow McFee and a tall man emerged naked from a creek and lay down on a blanket.

Goodluck lowered the binoculars.

"Widow lady, my ass," he said.

Late in the afternoon, Duffy, Cavill, and Sheriff Devens returned and stopped at the hotel where Goodluck was on the porch with coffee and a cigar.

"Well, we eliminated the three who live out of town," Duffy said. "How did you fair?"

"The widow McFee has a secret," Goodluck said.

"Let's get something to eat, and you can tell us all about it," Cavill said.

Over steaks in the hotel dining room, Goodluck told them about the widow McFee and the stranger at the creek.

"Mr. Goodluck, are you sure about this?" Devens said.

"Positive," Goodluck said.

"I think I'll have a talk with the widow McFee," Devens said.

"Don't do that, Sheriff. Not yet," Duffy said.

"What did you boys have in mind?" Devens said.

Goodluck tracked the buggy to the same spot the widow McFee drove to a day earlier. He, Duffy, Cavill, and Sheriff Devens dismounted and followed the tracks on foot.

They took up position a hundred yards from where the widow

McFee and the stranger spread out a blanket and ate a picnic lunch.

After they ate, the widow McFee and the stranger stripped and walked into the creek.

Duffy nodded and they walked to the blanket and looked at the widow McFee and the stranger, who were up to their necks in water.

"Mrs. McFee, a moment of your time," Duffy said.

The widow McFee and the stranger looked at Duffy, Cavill, Goodluck, and Devens.

"How dare you?" the widow McFee said.

Cavill bent over the stranger's clothes and removed the Colt revolver from the man's holster. "Look here, Jim," he said. "I think we might have us a match."

"The both of you get out of the water right now," Devens said.

"I'm a bit exposed here," the widow McFee said.

Cavill picked up the blanket. "Come out, or I come in," he said. "Which?"

Devens placed the widow McFee and the stranger, whose name was Morgan, into the cell opposite the cell occupied by Gordon.

"Good afternoon, ma'am," Gordon said.

The widow McFee rolled her eyes. "Oh, for God's sake," she said.

After test-firing Morgan's Colt at the gunsmith's shop and viewing it under the doctor's microscope, Duffy said, "Morgan is your man, Sheriff. No doubt."

"Let's go have a talk with him," Cavill said.

★ ★ ★ ★ ★

"I sent a wire to my office about you," Duffy said. "Want to see the reply?"

"Screw you and your reply," Morgan said.

They were in Devens's office. Morgan sat in a chair and looked up at Duffy.

"Just for the sake of clarity, my office sent a telegram telling us you are a professional gunman for hire," Duffy said.

"Like I said, screw you," Morgan said.

Cavill stepped forward and smacked Morgan across the face with so much force, it knocked Morgan to the floor.

"Say screw you again," Cavill said.

Duffy shook his head. "Jack, enough," he said.

Cavill grabbed Morgan and put him back in the chair.

"Now, we have enough evidence to guarantee you a rope, Mr. Morgan," Duffy said. "Or you can cooperate with us and do fifteen years. Which will it be?"

"Cooperate how?" Morgan said.

Duffy looked at Cavill and both men grinned.

"This is extraordinary," Governor Hale said.

"But true, Governor," Duffy said.

"Let me see if I understand this," Hale said. "Mrs. McFee hired Morgan to kill her husband, and they chose to do the deed the night after Gordon lost at cards to McFee. Is that correct?"

"Yes, but it's even more complicated than that," Duffy said. "According to Morgan, she hired him a month ago because she was tired of McFee beating her up all the time, and she and Morgan fell in love. They picked Gordon because he claimed McFee cheated him at cards."

"Oh, please," Hale said.

"Governor, I think a pardon for Gordon is in order," Duffy said

"I think I agree with you, Mr. Duffy," Hale said. "Sheriff, bring Mr. Gordon to my office at your convenience."

Duffy, Cavill, and Goodluck sat on the porch of the hotel with cups of coffee. All three men smoked Cuban cigars.

"That turned out rather well," Duffy said.

"It killed some time, anyway," Cavill said.

"The full moon is in two nights," Goodluck said. "I guess we'll know in three."

Sheriff Devens approached the hotel and joined the detectives on the porch. "Just thought I'd tell you boys the governor pardoned Joe Gordon, and a trial is set for one week to prosecute Mrs. McFee and Morgan. We owe you boys a debt of gratitude for saving an innocent man and putting the guilty parties on trial."

"Tell Gordon to stay out of card games," Cavill said.

"Join us for supper, Sheriff?" Duffy said.

Chapter Seventeen

Around midnight, Duffy, Cavill, and Goodluck sat on the porch of the hotel with Cuban cigars and small glasses of brandy.

They watched the full moon rise in the sky and illuminate the dark streets of Cheyenne.

"Maybe he gave it up after knowing he was being tracked," Cavill said.

"What do you think, Joseph?" Duffy said.

Goodluck glanced up at the moon. "I think tonight someone is going to die a horrible and painful death," he said.

Just south of the Wind River Indian Reservation, the small town of Lander, Wyoming, was asleep for the night.

Founded a few years earlier and named for General Frederick W. Lander, the town had a population of just two hundred residents, but was expected to grow quickly because oil explorers wanted to build the first oil well in Wyoming on that site in the near future.

Nestled in the Wind River Mountains, the town itself sat in the Wind River Basin and was chosen as the site to build an oil rig after much exploration.

Workers slept in tents, as the town had few amenities to offer. A dry goods store, a trading post, and a saloon was about it.

The saloon, such as it was, closed at one in the morning. Three men exited the saloon, drunk, and staggered toward their tents located a good hundred-fifty feet away.

The street was nothing more than mud from a recent rain. As the three men staggered through the mud, one of them slipped and fell. The other two men didn't seem to notice the fallen man and kept walking.

About a hundred feet from the tents, a large shadow appeared.

The two men stopped.

"Who goes there?" one of them said.

The large shadow moved in front of them.

"Show yourself, Goddammit," the other man said.

The shadow moved quickly and in the blink of an eye, one man's skull was cracked open from a powerful blow from a tomahawk.

The second man said, "Hey, what?" as the tomahawk struck him in the head.

The third man, still in the mud, looked up and saw the giant Indian holding scalps and immediately sobered up and screamed loud enough to wake every sleeping man in camp.

"Come on, Jim, let's go for a ride," Cavill said. "Sitting here on the porch writing letters is about the most boring thing I can think of."

"Do you want to lose your woman?" Duffy said.

"Of course not," Cavill said.

"Then finish your letter," Duffy said.

Cavill returned to his letter and tried to find words to say to Joey. Luckily, he was interrupted by Sheriff Devens, who approached the hotel porch.

"Boys, the governor wants to see you," Devens said.

"Jack, we'd best find Goodluck," Duffy said.

Duffy, Cavill, and Goodluck sat in chairs opposite Hale's desk.

"I received this telegram from the US Marshal assigned to

western Wyoming," Hale said as he slid the telegram across the desk. "Two men in Lander were scalped two nights ago. A third man witnessed the event."

"Where is Lander?" Duffy said.

"Just south of the Wind River Reservation," Hale said.

"How close can the railroad get us?" Duffy said.

"The town of Green River," Hale said. "From there it's a two-hour ride to Lander."

"Governor, get the train ready," Duffy said. "We'd like to be on it within the hour. And we'd like to use your telegraph to wire Charles Porter."

"How fast will this train go?" Duffy asked the conductor.

"With just the two cars, about sixty-miles an hour," the conductor said.

"Can we make Green River in five hours?" Duffy said.

"Easily," the conductor said.

Duffy looked at his watch. "So we can be there by five this afternoon?"

"Sure can," the conductor said.

"Let's go then," Duffy said.

The riding car proved to be quite comfortable, as it was the governor's personal car. Besides the luxurious seats, there was a kitchen for preparing meals, a conference table, and a bed where the governor could nap on a long trip.

Duffy prepared lunch in the kitchen for Cavill and Goodluck and also for the engineer and conductor.

After lunch, Duffy spread out a map on the conference table.

"Are you familiar with the Wind River Reservation?" Duffy said to Goodluck.

"Shoshone and Apache and Arapaho mostly," Goodluck said. "It's a large settlement. Good hunting and fishing. Cold winters. I spent some time there."

"How far is it from Landing?" Duffy said.

"On the map, a few hours' ride," Goodluck said.

"Why Landing?" Duffy said. "Unless he's hiding on the reservation. Can you get us in to see the elders?"

"We will see the elders," Goodluck said.

"Let's play some cards," Cavill said.

"Might as well," Duffy said.

"What in God's name is this shithole?" Cavill said when they stepped off the train.

"Jack, be polite," Duffy said.

"Are those adobe huts?" Cavill said.

"Jack, the only reason this town exists is to furnish water to the railroad," Duffy said.

"Let's get our horses and get going," Cavill said.

They retrieved the horses and mounted up.

"Goodluck, take us to Lander," Cavill said.

Two hours later, around seven in the evening, they arrived in Lander.

"What kind of town is it where the people live in tents?" Cavill said.

"It's not a town, not yet," Duffy said. "See that wood structure?"

"Yeah, what is it?" Cavill said.

"That's an oil rig," Duffy said. "They're drilling for oil."

They dismounted close to the rig, and a tall man wearing the badge of a US Marshal approached them.

"I'm Marshal Ralph Bevens," he said. "Are you the men the governor wired me about?"

"James Duffy and this is Jack Cavill and Joseph Goodluck," Duffy said. "First question, where are the bodies?"

"Follow me," Bevens said.

The followed Bevens through a long row of tents to the last tent.

"In there," Bevens said.

They entered the tent. The two bodies were covered in sheets on cots. Duffy removed the sheets. Both men had been scalped.

"Goodluck," Duffy said.

Goodluck examined each man. "Very efficient," he said. "He knows how to kill with one strike and scalp in one quick motion."

"I understand there's a witness," Duffy said.

"Jacob Farnsworth, a driller from back east," Bevens said. "He's employed by the oil rigging company. He and his . . . well, why don't you hear it from him."

Bevens led them to a large tent that served as a hospital. Farnsworth was in a cot, covered by a blanket.

"Mr. Farnsworth, these men are here to see you," Bevens said.

Farnsworth opened his eyes and looked at Bevens. "I need a drink," he said.

"You've had enough to drink," Bevens said.

"Marshal, where can we get some coffee?" Duffy said.

"The mess tent," Bevens said.

"Come on, Mr. Farnsworth, we're going to have a nice chat and get you sobered up," Duffy said.

Bevens cleared the mess tent so the detectives and he could have a private conversation with Farnsworth.

Duffy, Cavill, and Goodluck sat at a table with mugs of strong coffee. Bevens and Farnsworth sat opposite them.

Farnsworth attempted to roll a cigarette but his hands shook so much, he spilled the makings.

Bevens took the pouch and papers from Farnsworth and said, "Let me do it for you."

Bevens rolled a cigarette, gave it to Farnsworth, and lit it for him with a wood match.

"Mr. Farnsworth, please tell us what you witnessed," Duffy said.

Farnsworth inhaled on the cigarette, exhaled, and took a sip of coffee. "I should have stayed back east," he said. "But they offered just too damn much money and, like a fool, here I am."

"Tell us what happened," Duffy said.

"It was Pete's birthday. Me and Charlie took him for a few drinks," Farnsworth said. "We'd worked before on rigs in Texas and Oklahoma, you see. We didn't start out to get drunk, but we started toasting things, and before you know it, we were liquored up pretty good."

Farnsworth paused to sip coffee and inhale on the cigarette. Then he looked at Duffy through red, watery eyes.

"What happened next?" Duffy said.

"The saloon closed around one and we left," Farnsworth said. "It rained earlier, and I slipped in the mud on the way to the tents. That's when it happened. I looked up and I saw him. Big giant Indian standing there in front of Pete and Charlie. He was fast. Just like that, he killed Pete and Charlie with that short ax of his. I started to get up and saw he had a scalp in his hand. I screamed. After that I don't remember much, and I don't want to."

"Mr. Farnsworth, can you describe him at all?" Duffy said.

Farnsworth inhaled on the cigarette and said, "He was definitely an Indian. And big, like this fellow," he added, looking at Cavill. "I couldn't see his face much in the dark, but when he looked at me I could see his eyes in the moonlight. Evil is what I saw in them eyes. Pure evil."

Duffy, Cavill, and Goodluck had supper in the mess tent with Marshal Bevens.

"The governor has asked me to stay on here in Lander for a few more days as protection for these oil people," Bevens said. "But I doubt the killer will return."

"He hasn't yet returned to any site he's killed at so far," Cavill said. "He probably won't return here either."

"Tomorrow we'll visit the reservation and talk to the elders," Duffy said. "They might know something."

"There hasn't been any trouble with the tribes in ten years," Bevens said.

"I doubt there's any now," Duffy said. "This man is acting alone as far as we can tell."

"What's his game?" Bevens said. "What does he profit from all these killings? It's not like risking your neck to rob a bank. It's more like he's carrying out some sort of grudge or seeking revenge for something."

"I've thought about that," Duffy said. "Revenge seems unlikely, as he's killing people who have no connection to each other and, as far as we know, have never even met."

"A grudge is more realistic," Goodluck said.

"How so?" Bevens said.

"How old are you, Marshal?" Goodluck said.

"Forty."

"Forty years ago, most of Wyoming Territory still belonged to the Indians," Goodluck said. "The Crow, Arapaho, Lakota, and Shoshone roamed free in the mountains and high plains. Today these great people live on the reservation on land granted to them by a government that took it from them in the first place. I ask you, how would you feel?"

Bevens nodded. "Point well taken, Mr. Goodluck," he said.

"Marshal, we plan to leave after breakfast," Duffy said. "Is there a tent we can grab some sleep in?"

Duffy, Cavill, and Goodluck shared a large tent reserved for visiting officers of the oil company from back east.

Before turning in, they sat in chairs in front of the tent and smoked cigars.

"Joseph, what you said to Bevens at dinner, do you ever feel that way?" Duffy said.

"As a younger man, I used to," Goodluck said. "As I grew older, I realized that my people fought and killed each other far more than the whites ever did. As you grow older, you realize that peace is a greater gift than any treasures you could ever receive."

Duffy and Cavill looked at Goodluck.

"I wish my people felt that way," Duffy said.

Chapter Eighteen

After breakfast, Duffy, Cavill, and Goodluck mounted their horses. Bevens met them before they left.

"Can you tell the elders something for me?" Bevens said. "Tell them the government blames no tribal members for the actions of this one man."

"I'll leave that to Joseph," Duffy said. "It's more believable coming from him."

"I agree," Bevens said.

"Joseph, take us to Wind River," Duffy said.

The ride north took about three hours as they skirted the Wind River Mountains, which encompassed the southwestern part of the reservation.

A mile onto the reservation, they were met by a Shoshone hunting party of a dozen handsome warriors armed with Winchester rifles.

Goodluck left Duffy and Cavill and approached the hunting party. He spoke to the leader of the party in Shoshone.

After a few minutes, Goodluck returned.

"He said to follow them to Washakie," Goodluck said.

They followed the hunting party to a densely populated area of the reservation where Washakie lived in a fine cabin.

The leader of the hunting party dismounted and spoke in English. "Wait here," he said.

He entered the cabin and returned several minutes later with

Washakie on his arm. Somewhere between eighty and ninety years old, Washakie was dressed in pants, a colorful red shirt, and wore his long hair in braids.

Washakie motioned for Goodluck, Duffy, and Cavill to join him on the porch. They dismounted and stepped up onto the porch.

"I am Joseph Goodluck of the Mexican, Comanche people," Goodluck said. "These are my friends James Duffy and Jack Cavill. We are policemen."

"You are here about the killings in Wyoming," Washakie said. "The two men scalped in the Lander settlement where the men dig for oil."

"Yes," Goodluck said.

Washakie looked at the leader of the hunting part. "There is coffee on the stove. Bring us some," he said.

The leader nodded and entered the cabin.

"Who has a good smoke?" Washakie said.

Goodluck returned to his horse, removed four Cuban cigars from the box, and brought them to the porch. He gave one to Washakie.

"From the island country called Cuba," Goodluck said.

The leader returned with a tray and four mugs of coffee. After he gave each man a mug, he nodded and left the porch.

"Please sit," Washakie said.

Duffy, Cavill, and Goodluck took chairs.

"I have seen and done many things in my long life," Washakie said. "I traded with the French fur traders fifty years ago and learned their language. I fought wars against the whites and many tribes. I helped with the treaties at Fort Bridger and have traveled to Washington to speak with your leaders."

Washakie pulled a chain out from under his shirt to show the crucifix made of gold. "I have met with the minister John Roberts many times. He is a fine man, a good man, and we are friends."

Goodluck struck a match and lit Washakie's cigar.

"This man you are hunting, I know nothing of him," Washakie said. "I have spoken to all the tribal elders, and this man is a mystery. What he is doing makes no sense to anyone. What gain is there in senseless killings? I went to the fort to speak with the colonel, and they have no information on this man. I fear what he is doing will not end well for all concerned."

"Is it possible he is hiding somewhere on the reservation?" Goodluck said.

"If he is, he is a spirit," Washakie said. "Many warriors and the army have scouted the reservation for days without a sign of him."

"We will go to the fort to see the colonel," Duffy said.

"I will go with you," Washakie said. "It isn't far."

"Can you ride?" Duffy said.

Washakie smiled. "I have a buggy. A gift from your president on my last visit to Washington."

Goodluck drove the buggy, which was lavish and comfortable and had Washakie's name etched on the front in gold lettering.

The ride to the fort took about an hour. In honor of the great chief, the name of the fort was changed to Fort Washakie in 1878.

There was a plaque inside the buggy inscribing Washakie's help to the army in finding and defeating the Sioux after Custer's defeat at Bighorn.

Fort Washakie stood on about twenty-three acres of land and was home to two hundred soldiers, two lieutenants, two captains, and the commanding officer, Colonel West.

Every soldier not out on patrol turned out to watch Washakie's buggy ride to the center of the fort and park outside West's office.

West and two captains exited the office and stood on the porch. "Chief Washakie, this is an unexpected and pleasant surprise," West said.

"These men are police officers," Washakie said. "They are hunting the man scalping people in Wyoming."

"Come into my office," West said. "And will you stay for dinner?"

The captain filled five small glasses with brandy and gave one to West, Washakie, Duffy, Cavill, and Goodluck.

"To good health," West said.

All took a sip.

"Now, if I may ask, you men are from the detective agency out of Illinois, is that correct?" West said.

"That is correct, Colonel," Duffy said. "We are also federal constables with authority in all states and territory."

"Charles Porter, correct?" West said.

"He employs us," Duffy said.

"I've never met the man, but he is a legend in this part of the country," West said.

"Colonel, can you tell us anything about the man we're after?" Duffy said.

"I wish I could," West said. "I have three patrols of twenty men each out combing the reservation and mountains as we speak. So far there hasn't been a trace. The day after his attack, it rained, and any tracks he may have left were washed away."

"When do your patrols report back?" Duffy said.

"Late this afternoon," West said. "Probably before evening meal."

"You can stay the night in my cabin," Washakie said.

"That's a good idea, Chief. They can freshen up before supper," West said.

Washakie's cabin was built for his visits to the fort. It was large enough to house the usual six warriors he traveled with. Besides beds for seven, it had four bathtubs and an indoor toilet.

Duffy and Cavill shaved and then, along with Goodluck, took hot baths.

Cavill smoked a cigar as they soaked in the hot, soapy water.

"Goodluck, you've tracked for thirty years, how is it possible he is so evasive?" Duffy said.

"Whoever he is, he is a great tracker himself," Goodluck said. "And he has the element of surprise and time on his side. No one knows where he will strike and, by the time the victims are discovered, he's long gone. Even in Lander, by the time anybody knew what had happened, he was in the wind. Then he got lucky when it rained in the morning."

"Are you saying he scouts his attacks to make sure he can get away clean?" Cavill said.

"Yes, but also to strike fear into the people," Goodluck said.

"Well, he's certainly doing that," Cavill said.

"By the way, where is the chief?" Duffy said.

"Taking a nap before supper," Goodluck said.

A soldier suddenly entered the bathroom. "The colonel sent me to tell you the patrols have returned," he said.

Duffy, Cavill, and Goodluck met in Colonel West's office, along with the sergeants who led the patrols.

The sergeants made their reports.

"We tracked within fifty square miles," one of them said. "And saw no sign of anybody. We might as well have been tracking a ghost."

"We covered fifty square miles south of Lander," another

sergeant said. "We found nothing, but we did speak to three small ranchers who are pulling up stakes and putting their land up for sale."

The third sergeant said, "We covered every square inch of the reservation, including the mountains, and found nothing."

"Thank you, men," West said. "Stand down and get some rest. On the way out, tell the captain to get the next three patrols ready to leave in the morning."

After the sergeants left, West said, "I'll see you men as guests at my table for supper."

Duffy, Cavill, Goodluck, Washakie, and two captains sat at West's table for supper.

The large dining hall was filled to capacity with two hundred soldiers, and the noise level was high.

"Mr. Goodluck, you scouted for General Crook and Lieutenant Gatewood, am I correct?" West said.

"Yes, Colonel, and many others as well," Goodluck said.

"What advice can you share with my captains?" West said.

"You won't catch this man," Goodluck said. "He is long gone, and he knows you won't find him. He's accomplished what he set out to do, which is to spread fear among the white ranchers and farmers in Wyoming. I think the bigger question is why Wyoming? Why not some other state or territory? Why has he confined his actions to Wyoming? If he killed elsewhere, we would have heard about it by now."

Everybody looked at Goodluck.

"Of course, I'm just a scout," Goodluck said.

After supper, Duffy, Cavill, and Goodluck sat in chairs on the porch of Washakie's cabin.

Duffy and Goodluck smoked cigars.

"What you said tonight at supper, you are right," Duffy said.

"The soldiers won't catch him and neither will we, unless we get very lucky or he makes a mistake."

"He did make a mistake," Cavill said. "He was seen by Farnsworth and got lucky when the damn fool woke half the camp with his screaming."

"That's true," Duffy said. "So maybe he'll make another."

"We can't count on that," Goodluck said. "We will have to rely on patience to catch this man."

"Right now the only thing I'm counting on is a good night's sleep," Cavill said.

"That is a very good idea," Duffy said.

Chapter Nineteen

After breakfast with Colonel West, Goodluck drove Washakie's buggy back to the reservation, followed closely by Duffy and Cavill on horseback.

"What do you think, Jack?" Duffy said.

"Hell, I don't know, Jim," Cavill said. "We're chasing a renegade who's part ghost, for all I know. I'll tell you this much, though. He's not going to stop. He's enjoying himself too much to stop now."

By ten-thirty, Washakie was back at his cabin.

"Take coffee with me and rest your horses," Washakie said.

As Duffy and Cavill removed the saddles from their horses, a Shoshone warrior approached them. He spoke in Shoshone at Cavill.

"Goodluck, what's he talking about?" Cavill said.

"He says he admires your hat and wants to trade for it," Goodluck said.

"My hat?" Cavill said. "Tell him it's the only one I have, so it's no trade."

Goodluck told the warrior and the warrior responded in a harsh tone.

"He says you have insulted him," Goodluck said.

"Oh for . . . tell him I apologize, but he can't have my hat," Cavill said.

Goodluck spoke to the warrior. The warrior replied in anger.

"He says he will fight you for the hat and that if you refuse, everyone on the reservation will know you're a coward," Goodluck said.

"Jim?" Cavill said.

"Hold on," Duffy said and went up to the porch where Washakie sat in a chair with a cup of coffee.

"Chief, did you hear all that?" Cavill said.

"I heard," Washakie said.

"Chief, Jack is a professional fighter. An expert. Do you understand these words?" Duffy said.

Washakie nodded. "I understand," he said.

"You can't allow the warrior to fight Jack," Duffy said.

"He is what you would call a grandson," Washakie said. "And he needs to learn there are penalties for mistakes."

"Jack Cavill is a harsh penalty," Duffy said.

"Life is harsh," Washakie said. "It's best my grandson learns to tread lightly while he is still young."

"Okay," Duffy said.

Duffy returned to Cavill and Goodluck. "Goodluck, tell him Jack accepts his challenge," he said.

"Are you kidding me?" Cavill said.

"He's the chief's grandson, and Washakie wants you to teach him a lesson in humility," Duffy said.

Goodluck spoke to Washakie's grandson and the grandson nodded.

Cavill sighed as he removed his holster and slung it over the saddle on his horse. He placed his hat on the saddle horn and then removed his shirt and looked at the grandson.

The grandson looked up at the wall of muscle that was Cavill's chest, arms, and shoulders. He realized his mistake, but with at least thirty warriors watching, he couldn't back down.

"Goodluck, ask him if he's ready," Duffy said.

Goodluck spoke to the grandson and the grandson nodded.

"He's ready," Goodluck said.

Duffy sighed. "Jack, go ahead," he said.

Cavill walked to the grandson. The grandson assumed a wrestler's position. Cavill took a boxer's stance.

The grandson moved forward and tried to trip Cavill. Cavill jabbed the grandson twice in the face and then knocked him to the ground with a right hook that drew blood from his mouth.

Cavill stepped back to allow the grandson time to get up.

The grandson rose to his feet and spat blood.

Cavill knocked him down again with a stiff jab, followed by a powerful right hook.

Again, Cavill stepped back to allow the grandson time to stand up.

Slowly the grandson stood up, spat blood, and looked at Cavill.

The grandson screamed and charged Cavill, aiming for his legs. Cavill unleashed a powerful uppercut that struck the grandson flush on the jaw. The blow knocked the grandson to the ground where he rolled over backwards, looked up for a moment, and then passed out cold.

Cavill sighed, returned to his horse, and put his shirt back on, then his holster and hat.

"What took you so long?" Duffy said.

"Stupid kid," Cavill said.

Goodluck removed his canteen from his saddle and poured some water over the grandson's face. He spat blood and sat up.

Goodluck gave him a hand and yanked him to his feet.

The grandson walked to Cavill and nodded and then turned away.

"Wait a minute," Cavill said.

Goodluck spoke to the grandson, and the grandson paused.

Cavill opened a saddlebag and removed a new hunting knife in a polished leather sheath and held it out to the grandson.

"Goodluck, tell him it's a gift for his bravery," Cavill said.

Goodluck spoke to the grandson, and the grandson smiled at Cavill as he accepted the gift. As he walked away, the crowd gathered around the grandson to admire his new knife.

"Let's say goodbye to the chief and get moving," Duffy said.

Duffy, Cavill, and Goodluck joined Washakie on the porch.

"My grandson will think twice before he opens his mouth again," Washakie said.

"Chief, we need to get going," Duffy said. "But we will stop by and visit you when we can."

As they reached the edge of the reservation, an army rider approached them from the west.

"Hold up," Duffy said. "Let's see what he wants."

They waited for the rider to arrive. When he stopped his horse, he was flushed and exhausted.

Gasping, the soldier said, "Colonel West . . . wants you back at the fort. He said it's an emergency."

Duffy, Cavill, and Goodluck were surprised to see Marshal Bevens in Colonel West's office when they arrived.

The news wasn't good.

"This morning, county sheriff Jesse Alexander sent a deputy to Lander," Bevens said. "Fifteen miles south of Lander, a rancher, his wife, and their son were found murdered in their beds. Scalped."

"I'm sending a patrol with you," West said. "Captain Poule will lead the patrol."

"We'll ride to Lander and stay the night and get a fresh start come morning," Duffy said.

"Take whatever supplies you need from the mess hall," West said.

"Thank you, Colonel," Duffy said.

They reached the oil camp at Lander close to sundown.

The men were in the mess tent. A deputy sheriff met Bevens at the tents.

"The bodies were discovered when a neighbor happened to stop by on his way to get supplies," the deputy said. "He said something didn't seem right, so he stopped to check on his neighbors. He found them dead in their beds."

"Head back and tell the sheriff I'll be riding there in the morning with an army patrol," Bevens said. "And make sure the house isn't disturbed, even if he has to post deputies overnight."

The deputy nodded.

"I guess there's nothing to do until morning," Duffy said. "So let's grab some dinner and some sleep and leave at first light."

Chapter Twenty

They arrived at the ranch by nine in the morning. Two deputies were keeping watch on the porch.

"Everybody stays mounted until Goodluck inspects for tracks," Duffy said when they reached the picket fence that surrounded the house.

Goodluck dismounted and carefully inspected all tracks leading to the house. Then he looked at Duffy and Cavill.

"Have a look," he said.

Duffy and Cavill dismounted and walked to Goodluck.

"Barefoot tracks," Goodluck said. "Leading into and from the house."

"Jack, what size boot are you?" Duffy said.

"Fifteen," Cavill said.

"Take your right boot off and compare it to his," Duffy said.

Cavill sat on the porch steps and removed his right boot, and then placed his foot beside one of the tracks.

"I'd put him at about the same size foot," Duffy said.

"I'm going to see if I can pick up his trail," Goodluck said.

Duffy walked up to the porch. "Where are the bodies?" he said to the deputies.

"Buried out back," a deputy said.

Duffy and Cavill walked to Bevens and the army patrol. "Captain, there is no point in staying on with us," he said. "You might as well return to the fort."

"I agree," Captain Poule said and motioned to his men to

follow him as he rode away.

Bevens dismounted. "What now?" he said.

"That depends on Goodluck," Duffy said.

They waited in chairs on the porch for Goodluck to return. After about an hour, Goodluck rode back to the house and dismounted.

"He headed west to the Wind River Mountains," he said.

"I'll travel with you," Bevens said.

Duffy stood up. "Joseph, lead the way," he said.

Goodluck tracked the prints for several hours. Through green meadows, rocks and hills, and finally to the foothills of the Wind River Mountains.

They broke for lunch and to give the horses a two-hour rest.

While Goodluck built a fire and cooked lunch and Cavill tended to the horses, Duffy and Bevens studied a map.

"Do you know these mountains?" Duffy said.

"I've been stationed in Wyoming since seventy-seven," Bevens said. "On more than one occasion I've led a posse into the Wind River Range. It's some harsh terrain for sure. They stretch a hundred miles, and Gannett Peak is about thirteen thousand feet in height."

"A hundred miles of mountains to hide in," Duffy said. "Plus the Rockies and the Absaroka Range."

Bevens looked at Goodluck. "What do you think? Can you track him?"

"Any man can be tracked," Goodluck said. "Even this one."

"How much of a lead does he have on us?" Bevens said.

"Eighty miles, as the crow flies," Goodluck said.

"He's in no hurry then," Duffy said.

"No, but the horse he is riding is similar in size and weight to Jack's," Goodluck said. "If he wanted to, he could ride forty miles a day with no problem. Even longer."

"So he has no fear of being caught?" Duffy said.

"Judging from his handiwork, I'd say this man fears nothing," Goodluck said.

"Enough talk of him. Let's eat," Cavill said.

Close to nightfall, Goodluck dismounted and inspected the tracks. "He's turning more west," he said. "I'll scout ahead for a while."

While Goodluck scouted ahead, Duffy, Cavill, and Bevens made camp, got a fire going, and tended to their horses.

Goodluck returned an hour after dark. He dismounted and filled a cup with coffee and said, "He turned northwest about five miles from here."

"To the Wind River Mountains?" Duffy said.

"Weren't we there not long ago?" Cavill said.

"No, that secret outlaw camp in the Bighorn Mountains, remember?" Duffy said.

"I remember," Cavill said. "Maybe he hides out in the Wind River between killings?"

"We'll know for sure in a few days," Goodluck said.

"Have some grub. I'll tend to your horse," Cavill said.

In his bedroll beside the dwindling campfire, Cavill said, "Jim?"

"I know," Duffy said from his bedroll. "Joseph, are you awake?"

"I'm awake," Goodluck said, softly. "They're about three hundred yards west."

"Let's invite them in," Cavill said.

They built up the fire, then took their Winchesters with them and walked about a hundred feet to the west and stood in darkness.

"I'm not in the mood to bury anybody," Cavill said. "Anybody I kill will keep until morning."

Goodluck peered into the shadows cast by the half-moon. He held up two fingers and pointed to the edge of their camp.

Duffy, Cavill, Bevens, and Goodluck silently returned to their camp as two figures crawled on their bellies toward their saddlebags.

Cavill cocked the lever on his Winchester. "Best freeze, or I put a hole in you the size of a cannonball," he said.

Both figures froze in place.

"All right, both of you stand up near the fire and keep in mind four Winchesters are aimed directly at you," Duffy said.

The two figures slowly stood up beside the fire.

"For Christ sake, Jim, they're just kids," Cavill said.

The boy was about twelve, the girl just ten.

"Please don't hurt us," the boy said. "All we wanted was a little food."

"What in God's name are you kids doing out here in the dark?" Duffy said.

"Looking for food," the boy said. "My sister is awful hungry."

"Are you on foot?" Duffy said.

"Yes, sir," the boy said. "We were too afraid to go back after he killed our ma and pa. We just ran."

"All right, you kids sit by the fire," Duffy said. "We'll fix you something to eat. Then you tell us what happened."

Chapter Twenty-One

The boy's name was Adam. The girl's name was Sarah. They ate plates of beans, bacon, cornbread, biscuits, and a mixture of condensed milk and water.

"My ma and pa were really spooked over the ghost killer," Adam said. "They made us sleep in the loft the nights of the full moon. The steps pull up into the ceiling so no one can tell they're there."

"And someone killed your parents?" Duffy said.

Adam nodded as he shoveled in beans.

"When?" Duffy said.

"Three nights ago, when the moon was full," Adam said. "We heard him, but we was too scared to look. We waited until he was gone, and then we went down and saw what he did, and we just ran."

"You mean to tell me you kids have been out here for three days and nights?" Bevens said.

"We thought we were headed to Dubois, but we got lost," Adam said.

"Is that where you live?" Duffy said.

"Maybe five miles west," Adam said.

Duffy got out his map and held it close to the fire. "That's about twenty miles from here," he said.

"Sir, can my sister have some more? She's still awful hungry," Adam said.

"The both of you eat your fill," Duffy said.

While Adam and Sarah scooped more food from the pot, Duffy, Cavill, Bevens, and Goodluck walked twenty feet from the fire.

"We have to bury their parents," Duffy said.

"And then do what with them?" Cavill said.

"Take then to Dubois," Duffy said. "Somebody must know their parents."

"Okay," Cavill said.

They returned to the fire. "In the morning we'll take you to Dubois," Duffy said. "But first we need to bury your folks."

Adam nodded.

"You kids best get some sleep," Duffy said.

"I don't have an extra bedroll," Cavill said.

"We'll just sleep on the ground," Adam said.

"Our bedrolls will hold two," Duffy said.

Cavill looked at Duffy. "Mine won't," he said.

"I'll sleep with you," Sarah said to Cavill. "I'm little."

"I snore," Cavill said.

"So does my sister," Adam said.

"Well, that's just great," Cavill said.

Sarah stood up. She was the size of Cavill's leg. "Don't worry, I don't snore," she said. "My brother was just funning."

"She does talk in her sleep, though," Adam said.

"Well, that's just great," Cavill said.

Smelling coffee, Cavill opened his eyes with Sarah hugging him tightly about the waist.

"Oh, for . . ." Cavill said and wormed his way out of the bedroll.

Goodluck handed him a cup of coffee.

Duffy sipped coffee from a cup and grinned at Cavill. "How did you sleep, partner?" he said.

"Kid tosses more than flapjacks," Cavill said.

"Best wake them and get some food in them," Duffy said. "We got to cover twenty miles before this afternoon."

Cavill nudged Sarah with his boot. "Hey girl, wake up," he said.

Sarah opened her eyes, yawned, and looked at Cavill. "Morning, sir," she said.

"Cut the 'sir' stuff, and come eat some breakfast," Cavill said.

A few minutes later, Goodluck served up scrambled eggs with bacon.

"Where did you get the eggs?" Adam said.

"Nature," Goodluck said.

"I don't understand, sir," Adam said.

"Do you keep chickens on your ranch?" Goodluck said.

"In the henhouse," Adam said.

"And do you eat the eggs?" Goodluck said.

"That's why we keep them," Adam said.

"Wild chickens on the prairie lay the same eggs as the chickens in your henhouse," Goodluck said. "Remember that if you're ever lost again."

"Marshal, do you know the town of Dubois?" Duffy said.

"I do not, but I do know they're on the telegraph lines," Bevens said.

"All right, let's pack up and go," Duffy said.

Sarah looked at Cavill. "I'll ride with you," she said.

"Well, that's just great," Cavill said.

Sarah rode behind Cavill and hugged him tightly around the waist. Adam rode behind Duffy, and they made fifteen miles before one in the afternoon. Then they stopped for a quick lunch and to rest the horses.

Duffy checked his maps as they ate a light lunch of cornbread with leftover bacon.

"Adam, show me on the map where your ranch is," Duffy said.

Adam studied the map and then pointed to a road that led to his family ranch.

"About six or seven miles," Duffy said.

"I'll show you the road when we get there," Adam said.

"Well, let's get there," Duffy said.

They reached the road by two, and by two-thirty, they stopped in front of a modest ranch house Adam had pointed to on the map.

"Adam, you and your sister wait here," Duffy said.

Goodluck checked for prints while Adam and Sarah stayed with the horses. Duffy, Cavill, and Bevens entered the house.

The scene in the bedroom was ugly. Both mother and father had been scalped after their skulls had been smashed in. Sheets and blankets were caked in dried blood. Maggots were already crawling about the bodies.

"Oh, my God," Bevens said.

Cavill walked out of the room and went to the porch. Goodluck was on one knee, inspecting tracks.

"Joseph, take Adam and the girl to the henhouse to feed the chickens," Cavill said.

Two hours later, Cavill patted the last bit of dirt on the grave that held the mother and father.

Duffy and Bevens stood in the background and watched Cavill.

"I've never seen a man dig a grave so fast," Bevens said. "He didn't even take a sip of water."

"Jack has his ways," Duffy said. "He claims he doesn't care about anything, but that isn't true. It's just there is no telling what he's going to care about."

Cavill, Duffy, and Bevens walked around to the front of the

house. Cavill mounted his horse and then leaned over and pulled Sarah up to the saddle.

"Hold on tight," Cavill said.

Cavill yanked the reins and his horse galloped forward.

"Goodluck, best lead the way," Duffy said.

Chapter Twenty-Two

The town of Dubois was first settled by fur trappers in 1807 and had a population of about a thousand residents. Most of the commerce was in the way of supplies for the local ranchers.

Cavill stopped his horse in front of the sheriff's small office, dismounted, and helped Sarah down from the saddle.

Duffy, Goodluck, and Bevens dismounted next to Cavill, and Duffy helped Adam from the saddle.

The citizens on the street stared at Cavill as he tried the door to the sheriff's office and found it locked.

"He must be around here somewhere," Cavill said.

"He is," a woman on the sidewalk said. "At the general store."

"Wait here," Cavill said to Sarah.

"I want to go with you," Sarah said and took Cavill's hand.

Cavill lifted Sarah and held her in his left arm as he crossed the street.

"Like I said, there is no telling what Jack is going to care about," Duffy said.

Cavill reached the other side of the street and entered the general store. "I'm looking for the sheriff," he said.

A balding, potbellied man wearing a white apron behind the counter said, "I'm Sheriff Drucker."

"You're the sheriff?" Cavill said.

"Part time," Drucker said.

"Well Mr. Part-Time Sheriff, you're needed," Cavill said.

"I close the store at six, if you want to wait," Drucker said.

"You'll close the shop right now or get your skull thumped," Cavill said.

Drucker looked up at Cavill, realized what he was dealing with, and nodded.

From behind his desk, Drucker listened to Duffy as he explained what happened to Adam and Sarah's parents.

"I know them," Drucker said. "Good people. The kids go to school here."

"So what happens to them?" Cavill said.

"The county orphanage, I suppose," Drucker said.

Cavill looked out the window where Adam and Sarah waited on the sidewalk.

"To hell with that," Cavill said and walked out of the office.

Through the window, they watched Cavill lift Sarah in his arms, speak to Adam, and then walk away.

"Where's he going?" Drucker said.

"My guess is the telegraph office," Duffy said.

"Look, I'm sorry about their parents, but what else am I supposed to do with them?" Drucker said.

"I think my partner has an idea about that," Duffy said.

A few minutes later, Cavill returned, set Sarah down, and entered the office.

"Where is the nearest railroad?" he said.

"Riverton," Drucker said. "Three days' ride from here."

"What's on your mind, Jack?" Duffy said.

"I wired Joey," Cavill said. "I'm sending the kids to her ranch for now until we can think of something better."

"Jack, we're in the middle of a job," Duffy said.

"I know that," Cavill said. "Marshal Bevens, do you think you can take them to Riverton and put them on the train to Helena?"

Bevens looked at Drucker. "Can I rent a buggy in this town?"

Cavill sat on a bench with Sarah and Adam and told them about Helena. Duffy, Goodluck, Bevens, and Drucker stood on the sidewalk and watched.

"Why can't you take us?" Sarah said.

"I have to find the bad man who killed your parents," Cavill said. "As soon as I do, I'll be along to join you. In the meantime, my lady friend, Joey, will take care of you."

"But I want to be your lady friend," Sarah said.

"You have to grow up first, and for that you need a home," Cavill said.

Cavill stood up and looked at Drucker. "You got a hotel?"

"A boardinghouse," Drucker said.

"Show us," Cavill said.

The boardinghouse served a decent supper. Afterwards, while Adam and Sarah shared a bedroom, Duffy, Cavill, Goodluck, and Bevens took coffee on the porch.

Cavill and Goodluck smoked cigars with their coffee.

"I've been thinking," Bevens said. "I should escort the children to Helena. A long train ride isn't a journey kids that age should travel alone."

"Can you manage it?" Duffy said.

"The train stops in Cheyenne," Bevens said. "And I report only to the governor. The railroad line to Helena is nearly complete, so I can have them there in less than four days."

"We'll pay for the tickets and all expenses," Cavill said.

"We'll leave in the morning," Bevens said.

"So will we," Cavill said.

Chapter Twenty-Three

Sarah hugged Cavill tightly around the neck as he lifted her into the rented buggy.

"Now, you and your brother mind the marshal," Cavill said.

"Yes, sir," Sarah said.

"And the both of you mind Joey," Cavill said. "She is a good woman and will take very good care of you until I get there."

"Yes, sir," Sarah said.

"Marshal Bevens, thank you," Cavill said.

Bevens nodded and then rolled the buggy forward.

"Let's go see Drucker and load up on supplies," Duffy said. "And I'll send a telegram to Mr. Porter."

Joey really didn't need to go to Helena for supplies. Her foreman could have done that, but she rode along because she wanted to check the mail.

The last telegram from Cavill didn't say much, just that he was riding hard with his partner, James Duffy, and that he missed her.

Cavill wasn't a man of words. He more often than not stepped on his own tongue, but just the communication was enough.

In Helena, while her foreman picked up supplies, she stopped at the post office for the mail. A telegram for her was mixed in with the regular mail. It was from Cavill. She tore it open and read it quickly.

"What orphans?" she said aloud.

Miss Potts translated the telegram from Duffy and brought it immediately to Porter, who was in his office.

"They tracked the killer to the mountains," Porter said. "They're in Dubois and leaving for the Wind River Mountain Range. That's an impossible task, tracking through the mountains. But if anyone can do it, my money is on Mr. Goodluck."

Goodluck didn't pick up the trail until close to dark. They decided to make an early camp and rest the horses.

Studying his map, Duffy said, "Where the hell is he going?"

"Maybe the killer really does hole up in that secret hideout in the mountains between full moons?" Cavill said.

"There is something missing," Duffy said.

"How do you mean?" Goodluck said.

"Say he really is stark raving mad, which he probably is, what does he gain from these murders?" Duffy said. "There is no money in it for him. No one knows who he is, so there's no fame in it for him. What does he gain?"

"Maybe it's as simple as he just likes killing white people," Goodluck said.

"That could be, but I'm not buying he's just out to scare people in the territory with this full moon theory anymore," Duffy said. "There is something else at play that we're not seeing at this point."

"When we catch him, I'll be sure to ask him that very thing," Cavill said. "Right before I hang the son of a bitch."

"Jack, you keep that temper of yours in your back pocket," Duffy said. "We'll never get answers if you kill him."

"We were hired to find him and stop him, not play nursemaid," Cavill said.

"Stop him, yes. Kill him, no," Duffy said. "Look, I feel just as bad about what he did to Adam and Sarah's parents as you do, but our job is to find him and bring him to justice. If you plan on just executing him, then go home. We are not in the revenge business."

"Goodluck, can you find this son of a bitch?" Cavill said.

"I can find him," Goodluck said.

"Then find him," Cavill said as he lit a cigar.

Looking at the stars, Duffy tried to sleep, but the more he thought about the man they were after, the less likely sleep was to come.

"Hey, Jack, are you awake?" he said.

From his bedroll, Cavill said, "Barely."

"I don't want you to think I was berating you earlier," Duffy said. "I wasn't."

"I don't," Cavill said.

"Are you sure?" Duffy said.

"I'm sure, because I don't know what it means," Cavill said.

"It means—" Goodluck said.

"Oh, shut up," Cavill said.

Grinning, Duffy closed his eyes.

Chapter Twenty-Four

Goodluck tracked the murderer's movements all morning. By noon, they were in the foothills of the Wind River Mountains.

Goodluck dismounted to inspect what tracks he could find.

"He's turning northwest away from the mountains," he said.

"To where?" Duffy said.

Goodluck shook his head. "Only way to know is to follow," he said.

"Make camp. The horses need a rest," Duffy said.

While they ate a hot lunch of beans, bacon, coffee, and cornbread, Duffy studied his maps.

"Goodluck, you said northwest," Duffy said. "Look at the map."

Goodluck and Cavill sat beside Duffy and looked at the map. Duffy used his finger and traced a path northwest.

"Yellowstone," Goodluck.

"The park Wyoming and Montana are fighting over?" Cavill said.

"It's perfect to hide out in while he waits for the next full moon," Goodluck said. "Good game, good water, and lots of places to hide."

"We can make it in five days," Duffy said. "Which will give us two weeks until the next full moon."

"Have you been there, Joseph?" Cavill said.

"Many times," Goodluck said.

"What tribes are there left in Yellowstone?" Duffy said.

"Just hunting parties of Western Shoshone," Goodluck said.

"President Grant made it a public park back in seventy-two, forbidding anybody from building or residing on park grounds," Duffy said.

"If he's there, I'll track him," Goodluck said.

"Seven hours to dark," Duffy said. "Let's make the most of it."

"Up ahead," Goodluck said. "Five hundred yards. See that?"

"Hold up," Duffy said. He removed the binoculars from a saddlebag and scanned the horizon. "It's an overturned wagon."

"See anybody?" Cavill said.

"Too far even with the binoculars," Duffy said.

"Let's go have a look," Cavill said.

They rode to the wagon and dismounted. The wagon had held freight, and most of the wood boxes had spilled over. The horses that had pulled it were long gone.

"What do you think?" Duffy said.

Goodluck looked at the wagon tracks. "Something spooked the horses," he said.

Cavill knelt down and looked under the wagon. "There's somebody under there," he said.

"Is he alive?" Duffy said.

"Let's find out," Cavill said.

Cavill put his back to the wagon, squatted down, and grabbed the top of the cart. He took a deep breath and slowly stood up, lifting the cart off the ground.

"Grab his legs," Duffy said.

Goodluck and Duffy grabbed the man's legs and pulled him free of the wagon.

"Set it down, Jack," Duffy said.

Cavill lowered the wagon and looked at the man.

"It's an old man," he said.

"And still breathing," Duffy said. "Joseph, get some water."

"What's your name?" Duffy said.

"Douglas. Arthur P. Douglas."

"What happened, Mr. Douglas?" Duffy said.

Douglas was close to sixty, a wiry man with white hair and beard. "I was running my supplies from Little River to my place on Jackson Lake when a damn rattler spooked my horses and threw the wagon," he said. "I think my leg's broke."

Goodluck inspected Douglas's left leg. "It's a clean break," he said. "I can fix a tourniquet with some wood."

"My supplies," Douglas said.

"Don't worry about them now," Duffy said.

While Duffy and Goodluck made a splint from wood and bandanas, Cavill studied the overturned wagon.

He knelt in front of the wagon and gripped it from underneath.

"Jack, what are you doing?" Duffy said.

Cavill took a deep breath and used his legs and massive upper back strength to slowly lift the wagon off the ground until it stood upright. Then he pushed it forward, and it landed on its four wheels.

"Did I just see that?" Douglas said. "That big fellow just . . ."

"Mr. Douglas, how far to your place?" Duffy said.

"Maybe five or six miles from here," Douglas said.

"I'll hitch our horses to the wagon," Cavill said.

"My supplies," Douglas said.

"I'll load them back up," Cavill said.

Duffy and Goodluck rode in the front seat of the wagon, while Douglas sprawled out in back with his supplies.

Cavill rode his horse beside the wagon.

"This is a beautiful place you have, Mr. Douglas," Duffy said.

With Jackson Lake as a backdrop, there was a large log cabin, barn, corral, and forty acres of fenced-in land where Douglas raised horses for the army.

"I built every inch of it myself," Douglas said.

A handsome woman of about forty-five was hanging clothes on a line by the side of the house. She set the laundry basket aside and walked to the wagon.

"You old fool, what have you done?" she said.

"Oh, a damn rattler spooked the horses and flipped the wagon," Douglas said. "My left leg's broke. These men came along and saved my life, for sure. This is Mina, my wife. She's Shoshone."

"I'm James Duffy and this is Joseph Goodluck," Duffy said. "The big fellow is Jack Cavill."

"Can you bring him in the house?" Mina said.

Duffy looked at Cavill. "Jack?" he said.

Cavill dismounted, went to the wagon, scooped Douglas up into his arms, turned, and looked at Mina. "Ma'am," he said.

As Mina served beef stew, she looked at Douglas. "You old fool, get to bed. Your leg is broken," she said.

"My leg's been broke before," Douglas said. "Along with my right arm, lower back, and my short ribs. Give me two weeks and some good whiskey, and I'll be good as new."

"Old fool," Mina said as she placed fresh baked bread on the table.

"Sit and say your prayers, woman," Douglas said.

Mina made the sign of the cross and said a short prayer.

"She's Christian, as is her father, a Shoshone medicine man converted by the French," Douglas said.

"A little religion wouldn't do you any harm, you old fool," Mina said.

"Be thankful I'm alive, woman," Douglas said.

"I am, and to you gentlemen, I thank you for bringing my husband, the old fool, home," Mina said.

"You are very welcome," Duffy said.

"You'll be staying the night," Douglas said. "We have an extra bedroom that fits two and the big fellow can have the loft."

"Obliged," Duffy said.

"Say, how did you fellows happen by anyway?" Douglas said.

"We didn't just happen by," Duffy said. "We've been commissioned by Governor Hale to track the man who is murdering farmers and ranchers every full moon. We were tracking him to Yellowstone when we came across your wagon."

"I saw the newspapers in Little River about the latest," Douglas said. "Says he might be an Indian warrior of some kind. Is that true?"

"It's true," Goodluck said.

Douglas nodded. "Comanche?" he said to Goodluck.

Goodluck nodded. "My mother was Mexican Comanche. My father was from north of the Canadian River."

"What does he look like, this man?" Mina said.

"He's a big man, like our friend here," Goodluck said. "Rides a tall horse. That's all we know."

"Four days ago, after my husband left for supplies, I saw a big man on a large horse ride northwest past the house," Mina said. "It was too far to see his face, but he wore the sign of the Cherokee Nation on his horse."

"Cherokee?" Goodluck said. "Are you sure?"

"I am sure," Mina said.

"Did he see you?" Goodluck said.

"If he did, he didn't care and just rode on by," Mina said.

"Did you at least have the shotgun with you?" Douglas said.

"I did, but like I said, he didn't even look my way," Mina said. "He just rode at a steady pace, as if he had somewhere in mind to go."

"In the morning, can you show us where you saw him?" Duffy said.

Mina nodded. "There is plenty for seconds," she said.

After supper, Cavill helped Douglas to the porch for coffee.

"You belong in bed before you break your stupid neck along with your stupid leg," Mina said.

"Woman, we have guests," Douglas said. "Go see to their rooms."

Mina shook her head. "Does your leg hurt?"

"Of course it hurts. It's broke," Douglas said.

"Do you gentlemen have a watch?" Mina said.

"We all do," Duffy said.

Mina reached into the deep pocket of her apron and produced a pint bottle of whiskey. "For the pain," she said. "But when it is empty, please bring him to bed."

"Bless you, woman," Douglas said as he took the bottle.

"Don't blaspheme," Mina said.

After Mina went inside, Douglas added whiskey to the four coffee cups. "To your health, gentlemen," he said.

Cavill and Goodluck lit cigars.

"This is a fine place you have here, Mr. Douglas," Duffy said. "How long have you been here?"

"Going on twenty-five years," Douglas said. "Came here after we got married, when there was nothing. We built the cabin, barn, and every other thing you see. Every year we sell one hundred head of horses to the army at forty dollars a head. We grow our own vegetables on four acres and hunt what we need. We've had a good life out here."

"Any children?" Duffy said.

"Our daughter is at this fancy law school in Boston," Douglas said. "Our boy is a scout for the army out of Fort Laramie."

"Maybe you should send for him until that leg heals," Duffy said.

"Mina is probably writing the letter to him right now," Douglas said.

"How did you happen to marry a Shoshone woman?" Goodluck said.

"I came west as a young man," Douglas said. "Had nothing but ten dollars, a Hawken rifle, and some fur traps. This was before the war. I made friends with the Shoshone, and we trapped together on land that is now the reservation. That's how Mina and me met. We came here to get away from those that look down on Indians."

"Mr. Douglas, do people around here know your wife is Shoshone?" Duffy said.

"Pretty much everyone does. Why?" Douglas said.

"That could be the reason that man rode past your home and spared you," Goodluck said.

"I see," Douglas said. "Well, let's drink up. My leg hurts, and it's going to hurt a lot worse if I don't get to bed soon."

Chapter Twenty-Five

Duffy, Goodluck, and Cavill followed Mina to the edge of the ranch, where she'd seen the Indian ride past.

She dismounted her horse, as did Goodluck, and they looked at the tracks.

"It's him," Goodluck said. "I recognize the style of horseshoe and the horse's gait."

"I'd best be getting back to my husband," Mina said. "And thank you for making him a crutch."

Before breakfast, Goodluck went to the barn and made a crutch using wood and screws and padded the underarm rest with canvas filled with straw.

"You're welcome. Take care," Goodluck said.

"Bye, ma'am," Cavill said.

"Best keep that shotgun handy," Duffy said.

By noon, they had ridden past Jackson Lake and were on a clear path to Yellowstone Park.

They made camp and rested the horses for one hour while they ate a light lunch of cornbread, jerky, and water.

Duffy checked his maps.

"Joseph, have a look," Duffy said.

Goodluck sat beside Duffy and looked at the map.

"From where we are, it's sixty miles to Yellowstone," Duffy said. "How far ahead of us is he?"

"I put the tracks at five days old," Goodluck said.

"That's half of what it should be," Duffy said. "He's taking his sweet time, isn't he?"

"He's not in any rush, for sure," Goodluck said.

"Maybe he made a detour somewhere?" Cavill said.

"For what reason?" Duffy said.

"Maybe he had a few more people he wanted to kill?" Cavill said.

Duffy and Goodluck exchanged glances. "You could be right, but we can't worry about what we don't know. Let's get going, so we can make twenty miles before dark. Joseph, we'll follow you."

Around a campfire, Duffy, Cavill, and Goodluck ate plates of stewed beef with beans, cornbread, and coffee.

"The next full moon is less than two weeks away," Duffy said. "How far can a good horse ride in two weeks?"

"A stout horse like my Blue could cover five hundred miles, maybe a bit more," Cavill said.

"And he's on a stout horse," Duffy said.

"What are you driving at?" Cavill said.

Duffy took out his maps and spread them out near the fire. He touched Yellowstone Park with his finger.

"Five hundred square miles on a stout horse puts him anywhere from west of the Bighorns to south of what they call the Great Divide Basin," Duffy said. "That's dozens of towns, and hundreds of ranches and farmers to choose from. If we don't catch up to him in the next week, he'll strike again, and it could be anywhere."

Goodluck studied the map. "If he's in Yellowstone, he'll have to cross the Absaroka Mountains," he said. "Stout horse or not, that will slow him down some."

Duffy stared at the map. His mind was racing, trying to fit pieces of the puzzle together so they made sense.

"If he slows down, that would allow us to catch up," Cavill said.

"Of course," Duffy said.

Goodluck and Cavill looked at Duffy.

"Of course what?" Cavill said.

Duffy grabbed his saddlebags, pulled out the reports on the previous killings, and flipped through the pages.

"Jim?" Cavill said.

"Every time," Duffy said.

"Every time what?" Cavill said.

Duffy lowered the reports. "Every time he's killed, it's been within a day's ride to a town with a telegraph office so the news spreads quickly," he said. "He's not leaving it to chance that his victims will be found. He wants them to be found, and the best way to do that is pick populated areas with a telegraph line."

Cavill and Goodluck looked at the map.

"He'll stay west of the Bighorn Mountains and pick his next victim close to a town with a telegraph line," Duffy said. "What towns do we know are on the line?"

"Cody, Dubois, Riverton, Lander, and every town along the railroad line west of Cheyenne," Cavill said.

"If he's in Yellowstone, he'll pick a target close to a telegraph line," Duffy said. "Somewhere north and close."

"Goodluck glanced up at the sliver of a moon. "We'll be in Yellowstone tomorrow," he said.

"Yeah, but where will he be?" Cavill said.

"Waiting," Goodluck said.

"For what?" Cavill said.

"The next full moon," Goodluck said.

Chapter Twenty-Six

By late afternoon the next day, Goodluck led Duffy and Cavill into Yellowstone Park. Their elevation was high, and mountains surrounded them.

"There's a meadow not far from here," Goodluck said. "It's a good place to camp."

In the meadow, near dark, they made camp.

"We'll need to hunt some game," Duffy said. "We're low on meat."

As they cooked supper, Duffy studied his maps. "The railroad built a stop in the town of Livingston on the Yellowstone River north of the park," he said.

"What for?" Cavill said.

"My guess is to take people to the park for sightseeing," Duffy said.

"What sights?" Cavill said. "There's nothing here but grass and mountains."

"Back east they see nothing but cement and buildings," Duffy said. "They'll come a long way to see grass and mountains."

"Come morning, I'll scout ahead for tracks and do some hunting," Goodluck said. "If he's still here, I'll know."

Hard rain had washed away any tracks shortly after they entered the park, so Goodluck was scouting on instinct and experience.

"Let's build up the fire," Duffy said. "The night air is colder in these mountains."

After eating, they spread out their bedrolls beside the fire and watched as millions of stars blinked overhead.

In the distance, a low, savage rumbling noise sounded.

"What is that?" Cavill said.

"Wolves," Goodluck said. "Eating."

A little while later, the wolves howled in the darkness.

"Well, this is just great," Cavill said. "A little music to put us to sleep."

The temperature before dawn was close to freezing, but as the sun rose, the air quickly warmed. They made a fire and put on a pot of coffee. Then Goodluck dug out his bow and arrows from his gear and went hunting.

As he drank his coffee, Cavill smoked a cigar. "The scalper might be long gone by now," he said. "Waiting out the full moon for his next victim."

"That's twelve days from now," Duffy said. "My guess is he won't expose himself until the last minute, when he strikes. If Goodluck can't pick up his trail, we can go to Livingston and wait for news over the telegraph."

"And buy some damn warmer jackets," Cavill said.

Joey waited at the stagecoach depot, not knowing how the children would arrive. She had stopped at the post office, but there were no letters or telegrams from Cavill, so she had no real idea what to expect.

Much to her surprise, a United States Marshal driving a buggy with the children arrived and parked at the depot.

The marshal stepped down. "I'm United States Marshal Bevens, ma'am," he said. "Would you be Josephine Jordan?"

"I am," Joey said.

"You're exactly as Mr. Cavill described," Bevens said.

"And where is Mr. Cavill?" Joey said.

"At the moment, I don't know," Bevens said. "When I left him and his partners near Dubois in Wyoming, they were pursuing a man wanted for multiple murders. They were headed west at the time. That's when Mr. Cavill asked me to deliver the children to you."

"I see," Joey said. "Well, stand up, you two. Come here and let me have a look at you."

Adam and Sarah stepped down from the buggy and walked to Joey.

"Jack told us to call you Miss Joey," Adam said.

"Did he? What else did he tell you?" Joey said.

"He said you were very pretty," Sarah said. "And you are."

"Ma'am, I have to get back to Wyoming," Bevens said as he placed Adam and Sarah's bags on the ground. "Oh, almost forgot. This is for you."

Bevens reached into his jacket pocket and then handed Joey a sealed letter.

"Thank you, Marshal," Joey said.

After Bevens rode away, Joey looked at Adam and Sarah. "Now what am I going to do with you two?" she said.

"Jack said you'd say that," Adam said.

"Get in my buggy," Joey said. "And don't forget your bags. You can tell me what else Jack said on the way."

"I found a campfire just over this hill," Goodluck said. "The rain washed away any tracks, but I think it's from five nights ago."

They reached the top of the hill and looked down at a large pasture full of bison grazing on the tall grass.

"Will you look at that," Duffy said. "Must be two hundred of them."

"When I was a boy, there were two million of them," Goodluck said.

"Let's keep going until noon, and then we can eat those chickens you hunted this morning," Duffy said.

Goodluck kept them on a northern path that took them through the pasture, over some hills and rocks, and into another pasture.

They passed another herd of bison and stopped when they saw a hunting party of Western Shoshone Indians skinning a bison they'd hunted.

"Let's go say hello," Duffy said.

They rode across the pasture to the Western Shoshone warriors. Goodluck spoke to them in Shoshone.

A warrior of about thirty, dressed in dungarees and a blue shirt, said, "Yes, we speak English. I am called Moses of the Shoshone people."

"I am Joseph Goodluck, and these are my partners, James Duffy and Jack Cavill," Goodluck said. "We are lawmen, and we are tracking a Cherokee outlaw through the park."

"Cherokee?" Moses said. "We stopped in Livingston to alert the authorities we would be hunting in Yellowstone. We are allowed, but we like to tell them when we hunt for bison. There was much talk of the ghost killer in Wyoming."

"That is the man we are after," Goodluck said.

"No one said he is Cherokee," Moses said. "Not even your newspapers."

"We only recently discovered it," Goodluck said.

"In your travels, have you seen such a man?" Goodluck said.

"No, but we did see a camp where a man stayed for several nights," Moses said. "He made big prints and rode a very large horse."

"Where?" Goodluck said.

"A day's ride from here in the magic springs," Moses said.

"Magic springs?" Cavill said.

"The geysers," Duffy said.

"Can you show us?" Goodluck said.

Moses nodded. "Let me cut out some meat for the journey," he said.

Joey parked the buggy in front of the ranch house and stepped down.

"This is your house?" Adam said.

"This is home," Joey said. "Come on, I'll show you your rooms."

After her father died, Joey moved into his room, which left three vacant bedrooms. She brought Adam and Sarah into the house and they looked around in wide-eyed wonder at so lavish a home.

"This is your room, Adam," Joey said. "Sarah, yours is just down the hall."

"We each have our own room?" Adam said.

"Yes," Joey said. "Now settle your things, and I'll ask the cook to start lunch."

"You have a cook?" Adam said.

"This is a working ranch," Joey said. "I don't have time to waste in the kitchen."

Joey showed Sarah her room and then went to the study to read Cavill's letter.

Dear Joey, It's me Jack, the letter began.

Joey had to look up and smile. "No kidding, it's you," she said aloud.

I didn't know what else to do with these two except to ask you to look after them until I arrive, Jack wrote. *Their parents were killed by the outlaw we're pursuing, and I couldn't see sticking them in some state-run orphanage. They are good kids and very brave. Please look after them until I come back and we can figure out what to do with them. Yours, Jack. PS- I love and miss you a lot.*

Joey folded the letter and tucked it away in her desk. "Big dope," she said. "Come back in one piece."

"Just how damn big is this Yellowstone?" Cavill said as they made evening camp.

"Larger than Rhode Island or Delaware," Duffy said.

"Noon tomorrow, we will reach where he camped," Moses said.

"Let's get a fire going and see to the horses," Duffy said.

With the fresh bison meat, they made stew and had bread and coffee with it. After eating, they drank coffee and Cavill and Goodluck smoked cigars.

"This Cherokee, he has killed many men," Moses said.

"And women," Duffy said.

"He kills women?" Moses said.

"He hasn't started killing children yet that we know of, but it wouldn't surprise me none if he did," Cavill said.

"They say he kills only when the moon is high," Moses said.

"It's true," Duffy said. "The nights of the full moon are when he kills."

"The high moon is when the coyote, wolf, and panther are most successful," Moses said. "Ancients believed in the spirits of these animals."

"Those animals kill for food," Duffy said. "This man is killing for sport. If we don't stop him soon, there won't be a farmer or rancher left in the whole territory."

Duffy stared into the campfire as he thought about his own words.

"Jack?" Duffy said.

"Yeah."

"That's what this crazy son of a bitch wants," Duffy said.

"What?" Cavill said.

"To drive every farmer and rancher out of Wyoming," Duffy said.

Chapter Twenty-Seven

As he entered the office, Porter stopped at the desk of Miss Potts. "Any word from Duffy and Cavill?" he said.

"Not since the last telegram," Miss Potts said.

Porter sighed and went to his office. He scanned the mail, wrote a few letters, and then picked up the cone.

"Miss Potts?" he said.

"Yes, Mr. Porter?" she replied.

"A moment, please."

Miss Potts entered the office.

"Book two tickets to Cheyenne on the morning train for tomorrow," Porter said. "All this sitting around is driving me mad."

"Two tickets?" Miss Potts said.

"You're my personal assistant, aren't you?" Porter said. "Tell whoever is working our telegraph to reply to me at the governor's office in Wyoming, starting tomorrow night."

"Yes, Mr. Porter," Miss Potts said.

"Why are we going back to town?" Adam said as he helped Sarah into the buggy.

"To get you some proper clothes," Joey said. "The both of you look like Chicago street beggars."

Joey tugged the reins and steered the buggy to the road.

"What's a street beggar?" Adam said.

"What's Chicago?" Sarah said.

"Never mind," Joey said. "Can either of you ride a horse?"

"Our pa raised horses," Adam said. "Our place ain't nothing like yours, but we can both ride."

"Then we'll add some riding clothes to the list of what you'll need," Joey said.

"What's riding clothes?" Sarah said.

"You'll find out," Joey said.

"Miss Joey, what about our place in Wyoming?" Adam said.

"We'll find out about that in town," Joey said.

Goodluck inspected the campsite, the footprints, and tracks made by the horse.

"It's him," he said. "Same tracks, same boot prints."

"How long ago?" Duffy said.

Goodluck inspected charred wood in the circle of stones and felt the ashes. "No more than five days," he said.

Duffy turned to Moses. "We'll have lunch and then you can return to your people," he said. "And we thank you for your help."

"Why do I need dresses for?" Sarah said.

They were in the large general store in Helena in the section for clothing.

"Because you're a girl," Joey said.

"You're a girl and you're wearing pants," Sarah said.

"I'm wearing work clothes," Joey said. "When I'm not working, I wear dresses."

"You look funny in that dress," Adam said.

"I do not," Sarah said. "Girls wear dresses, you stupid."

"Adam, go pick out some work clothes and some dress clothes," Joey said.

"What's the difference?" Adam said.

Joey sighed. "Never mind," she said. "We'll take care of you after we finish with your sister. And then we'll go see Mr. Cranston."

"Who is Mr. Cranston?" Adam said.

"A lawyer," Joey said.

"What is that?" Cavill said.

They'd ridden for several hours and stopped as they entered the hot springs.

"A geyser," Duffy said.

"What's it do?" Cavill said.

"Let's give the horses a rest and watch," Duffy said.

As they sat with their backs against their saddles, Cavill said, "It just looks like a bubbling hot . . ."

And suddenly the geyser shot boiling hot water a hundred feet into the air.

"Now you know what it does," Duffy said.

The spray of boiling water lasted for about two minutes before it calmed down.

"That's one of the sights people come from back east to see," Duffy said.

"It will never catch on," Cavill said. "Who would travel thousands of miles just to see some hot water. Let's keep going until dark."

"Joseph, can you pick up his trail?" Duffy said.

"You look very nice in that dress, Sarah," Joey said.

"Why do I have to wear a dress just to eat supper?" Sarah said.

"It's what a young lady does," Joey said. "Adam, you also look very nice in those new clothes."

"Yes, ma'am," Adam said.

"Please sit down so Mr. Dent can serve dinner," Joey said.

Dent, the cook for the house as well as for the men in the

bunkhouse, entered the dining room.

"You're a man," Sarah said.

"Men can cook," Joey said. "Mr. Dent was a chef in a big restaurant in the city of Saint Louis before coming here. And he's made a special treat for you for dessert. Ice cream."

"What's ice cream?" Sarah said.

"You'll find out," Joey said.

Duffy and Cavill made camp before dark, while Goodluck scouted ahead. Duffy made a fire and put on a pot of coffee while Cavill tended to the horses.

"We need water," Duffy said.

"I'll see what I can find," Cavill said.

"We passed a stream about five hundred yards to the east," Duffy said.

Cavill tossed his saddle on Blue and took the canteens. "I won't be long," he said.

While Cavill was away, Goodluck returned.

"Jack went for water," Duffy said.

Goodluck removed his saddle and then grabbed a cup of coffee. "His tracks have turned northeast," he said.

Duffy took out his maps. "Show me," he said.

Goodluck studied the map. "Here," he said.

"I think he's headed for the Yellowstone River toward Livingston," Duffy said.

"Waiting for the next full moon," Goodluck said.

"I'll get some supper going," Duffy said.

"You do that," a voice behind Duffy and Goodluck said. "And no beans. I hate beans."

Duffy and Goodluck turned and looked at two men holding Henry rifles on them. They were filthy, dressed in buffalo hide, and had the look of poachers about them.

"Toss them pistols to the dirt," one poacher said. "And slow, like winter molasses."

Duffy and Goodluck looked at the poacher.

"You deaf?" the poacher yelled.

Duffy and Goodluck removed their sidearms from the holsters and tossed them to the ground.

"Tie them up, Pip," the poacher said.

"With what?" Pip said.

"They got rope on their saddles. Use that," the poacher said.

Pip went to the saddles for rope.

"Now, you two get on your bellies," the poacher said.

Duffy sighed and slowly got down on his stomach.

"Injun, are you deaf," the poacher said. "On your belly."

Goodluck got down next to Duffy.

"Now we're gonna take them fine horses and everything else you got and be on our way," the poacher said.

"You won't get very far," Duffy said.

"Why's that?" the poacher said.

Behind the poacher, Cavill shoved his field knife deep into the poacher's back. The poacher dropped the Henry rifle and slumped to his knees.

About to tie Duffy's hands, Pip dropped the rope and reached for his Henry rifle.

Cavill drew his Colt and shot Pip twice in the chest.

Duffy sat up and looked at the poacher.

"That's why," Duffy said.

The poacher looked at Duffy and then fell over dead.

"What do you want to do first, make supper or bury these two pilgrims?" Cavill said.

Joey, Adam, and Sarah took ice cream on the front porch.

"I never had ice cream before," Adam said.

"I wish Ma could have had ice cream," Sarah said.

Adam lowered his bowl. "Yeah," he said.

"Miss Joey, are Ma and Pa in heaven like they told me about?" Sarah said.

"I'm sure they are, Sarah," Joey said. "I'm sure they are looking down at you right now and are pleased at how brave you both are."

Sarah set her bowl on the table and hugged Joey tightly around the neck and started to cry.

"This must be so hard on you," Joey said. "The both of you."

"I hope Jack finds that man and makes him pay for what he did," Adam said.

Joey stroked Sarah's hair. "I have every faith in Jack that he will do just that," she said. "You wait and see."

As they ate a supper of venison stew with beans and cornbread, Duffy said, "Goodluck found his tracks headed northeast. I think he's headed toward the river out of the park."

"Good," Cavill said. "I'm sick of this place."

"I think he already has a victim in mind," Duffy said. "He's going to leave the park and hole up close and wait for the next full moon."

"If we can catch him, we can stop him," Goodluck said. "For that to happen, we need to ride forty or more miles a day, and he needs to hold his course. If he suspects he's being followed, he'll speed up or go into hiding."

"What do you think, Jim? Can that nag of yours do forty miles a day?" Cavill said.

"You just watch him," Duffy said. "Now I suggest we get some sleep and leave before dawn."

Chapter Twenty-Eight

"As I thought, he's crossed the river," Goodluck said. "I put the tracks at four days old."

Duffy spread out his maps. They were having lunch at the bank of a tributary of the Yellowstone River in the Absaroka Mountains.

"We're north of Livingston and the railroad," Duffy said. "I believe we're in Montana now, so he'll have to head south if he's to keep killing in Wyoming. Goodluck, you and Jack keep following the tracks. I'll go to Livingston, send a wire to Mr. Porter, pick up fresh supplies, and I'll catch up to you in a day or so."

"I'll leave markers for you to follow," Goodluck said.

"I'll leave right after lunch," Duffy said.

"Pick us up some extra cigars," Cavill said. "We're running low."

"I didn't expect to see you in Wyoming, Charles," Governor Hale said when Porter and Miss Potts entered his office.

"I like to get out of the office once in a while," Porter said. "Have my men reported in at all, Governor?"

"Not for a while, I'm afraid," Hale said.

"Miss Potts and I will stay in Cheyenne until we hear from them," Porter said. "We'll be at the Doral Hotel."

"Let's have dinner tonight, Charles," Hale said. "Seven

o'clock at my residence."

"We'll be there," Porter said.

Herb Cranston had been Joey's father's attorney for twenty years before her father died. He was a close family friend and confidant, and she trusted him totally.

Adam and Sarah waited in the reception office with his secretary while Joey spoke with Cranston privately.

"It must be very hard on those kids, Joey," Cranston said. "I'll see what I can do about the ranch in Wyoming. Technically it's their property, but if the taxes aren't paid, it will be confiscated by the government and sold at auction."

"Can you find out what the taxes are and if there is a mortgage?" Joey said.

"I can send some telegrams," Cranston said. "What are you thinking?"

"Selling the ranch and putting the money into an account for the children," Joey said.

"And the children?" Cranston said.

"I don't know," Joey said. "I'll wait until Jack returns, and we'll discuss it."

"Remember when you were nine?" Cranston said.

Joey had found a baby owl with a broken leg and nursed it back to health in the barn. After six months, the owl was large enough and well enough to fly away on its own, but by then Joey had become so attached to the owl she refused to let it leave the barn. When her father and mother finally convinced her to release the owl, she was heartbroken for months.

"I remember," Joey said.

"I'll get back to you as soon as I have some information," Cranston said.

Livingston was a town of about two thousand residents,

established by the Northern Pacific Railroad as a destination place for visitors to Yellowstone Park.

The town was clean, modern, and built around the idea of making visitors to the park feel comfortable and welcome.

Duffy drew stares as he rode down Main Street. His clothes were dirty, a week's growth of beard covered his face, and his Smith & Wesson sidearm seemed very out of place.

He dismounted in front of the sheriff's office, a red brick building, and tied Bull to the hitching post.

The sheriff was behind his desk, and he looked at Duffy as he entered the office.

"Can I help you, young fellow?" the sheriff said.

Duffy set his wallet on the desk. "James Duffy, detective with the Illinois Detective Agency," he said.

The sheriff scanned the identification.

"How can I help you, Mr. Duffy?" the sheriff said.

"Can I buy you a cup of coffee? It's a long story," Duffy said.

"Looking the way you look, you'd scare half the tourists in town," the sheriff said. "Pull up a chair, Mr. Duffy. I got some hot coffee on the stove."

Goodluck stuck the cross he made from two branches into the dirt beside their camp.

"That's three for Jim to follow," he said.

"I should have asked him for the maps before we left," Cavill said.

"Can you read a map the way he does?" Goodluck said.

"No, but I figured you can," Cavill said.

"We crossed back into Wyoming," Goodluck said. "Tomorrow I will pick up the killer's trail again and leave more markers for James."

"Did you understand all that stuff Jim was talking about?" Cavill said. "All that stuff about square miles?"

"Yes," Goodluck said. He opened his saddlebags, removed a folded map, and spread it out in front of the campfire. "This is where we are right now," he said.

"In the middle of nowhere," Cavill said.

"Yes, but not far away from here there are many ranchers and small farmers nestled between the mountains," Goodluck said.

"If he rides forty miles a day, how far can he ride before the next full moon?" Cavill said.

"Sixteen hundred square miles of territory," Goodluck said. He traced a circle on the map with his finger. "Here to here," he said.

Cavill studied the map. "If he wants the news of his next victims to travel fast, he wants to be near the telegraph," Cavill said. "If he travels south, he has to cross the Owl Creek Mountains and the telegraph would be where? Fort Washakie on the reservation."

"Possibly Green River with the railroad?" Goodluck said.

Cavill lit a cigar and leaned back against his saddle. "We're just spitting in the wind here. We got no idea where the hell he's headed and who he's going to kill next."

"We've made ground," Goodluck said. "The last tracks were three days old. He might have selected his next victim and is waiting for the full moon."

"Maybe so, but if we speed up, we can catch him before he kills again," Cavill said.

"My friend, this man is Cherokee," Goodluck said. "There are only two ways to catch him. The first one is by luck. The second is if he wants you to."

"If that's true, then what the hell are we doing out here?" Cavill said.

"Hoping for luck," Goodluck said.

Cavill rested his back against the saddle and lit a cigar.

Goodluck reached into his saddlebags, removed a paperback novel, and started to read beside the fire.

"What are you reading?" Cavill said.

"The Count of Monte Cristo."

"What's it about?"

"A man hoping for some good luck," Goodluck said. "Just like us."

Duffy and the sheriff exited the telegraph office and walked along the wood sidewalk to the hotel where Duffy had registered for the night.

"Give me an hour and a half to grab a shave and a bath, and I'll buy you dinner at the hotel," Duffy said.

"See you about nine then," the sheriff said.

"Charles, I just don't know what to do about this situation," Hale said. "As governor, I could call upon the army to scour the countryside, but I don't think that would do any good. Lord knows, what marshals I do have can't handle their workload as it is."

They were in the study of Hale's residence with brandy and cigars.

"Give my boys until the next full moon," Porter said.

There was a knock on the door. A moment later it opened, and Miss Potts walked in.

"Miss Potts, I thought you went back to the hotel," Porter said.

"I did, but this rather lengthy telegram arrived from Mr. Duffy," Miss Potts said, and she handed the telegram to Porter.

Porter read the telegram quickly and then passed it to Hale.

Hale read it and looked at Porter. "Let's have another brandy, Charles," he said.

"Miss Potts, would you join us?" Porter said.

"I could use one, too," Miss Potts said.

"Everybody in these parts knows about the full-moon killings," the sheriff said. "Folks are wondering if the killer'd move north into Montana."

"He hasn't so far," Duffy said. "But anything is possible. I guess we'll find out the next full moon."

After a shave, a bath, and a change into the last pair of clean clothes in his saddlebags, Duffy and the sheriff had steaks in the hotel restaurant.

"What does this man want?" the sheriff said. "Nobody just kills for the sake of killing, not even a crazy person."

"This man is not crazy," Duffy said. "He's highly skilled at tracking, hunting, stalking, and avoiding detection. Why he's doing what he's doing is anyone's guess."

The sheriff nodded. "When are you leaving?"

"As soon as I get supplies in the morning," Duffy said.

"I guess there's not much I can do besides wish you good luck," the sheriff said.

"I have to ask myself what a Cherokee warrior hopes to gain by this bloodshed," Hale said.

"I can't answer that right now, Governor," Porter said. "We'll just have to wait for the next communication from my men."

"You'll be staying in Cheyenne then?" Hale said.

"Until the next full moon, at least," Porter said.

Chapter Twenty-Nine

After picking up his clean clothes from the hotel laundry and buying supplies at the general store, Duffy left Livingston before nine in the morning and rode south into Wyoming.

He found his own tracks, and then followed the trail left behind by Goodluck and Cavill.

By noon, Goodluck and Cavill were deep in a canyon halfway through the Absaroka Mountains.

"We'll camp here and wait for Jim," Goodluck said. "He should be able to reach us by late morning tomorrow."

"I don't fancy sitting around doing nothing," Cavill said.

"I'm going hunting. Make a fire," Goodluck said. "After that, we'll scout ahead and return by nightfall."

Close to sundown, Duffy found the third cross left behind as a marker by Goodluck and Cavill. The trail led southeast through the Absaroka Mountains.

He made camp, built a fire, and tended to Bull as supper cooked.

As he ate supper, Duffy kept hearing the sheriff's words in his mind. *What does this man want?*

He took out his maps and notes. Where was the closest town with either the railroad or telegraph lines? If he kept traveling south toward the reservation, he could strike in the Lander or

Green River area again and have access to both railroad and telegraph.

Where else?

Thermopolis, where the hot springs was located, drew thousands every year to bathe in the hot mineral water.

That was a possibility.

Easy targets, the railroad, and access to telegraph lines nearby to spread the news.

Duffy realized the only way to stop the man was to catch him in the act. This man was not the kind to be intimidated by the law or the notion of punishment for his crimes.

Duffy cleared his mind, took out his writing paper, and penned a letter to Sylvia.

Goodluck killed three chickens for supper and Cavill gathered twelve eggs from their nests for breakfast.

Before roasting the chickens on a spit made of sticks, they took a bath in a stream they discovered a few hundred yards away. Cavill brought his razor and took a shave before joining Goodluck in the water.

They each had one clean shirt to put on after bathing. Then they built a fire and put the chickens on to roast.

"We'll stay put in the morning to allow Jim to catch up to us, but if you could wait, I'd like to scout ahead," Goodluck said.

"He'd better have remembered our cigars," Cavill said. "I'm down to just four."

"Jim never forgets anything," Goodluck said.

Trent looked across the formal dining table at his daughter and said, "It's been weeks, Sylvia. How much longer are you going to pout like a child?"

"How dare the man speak to me that way?" Sylvia said. "I can't wait for him to return so I can throw his ring in his face, the buffoon."

"That's your decision, but James is as fine a man as I've even known," Trent said. "He'll be a lawyer soon, and might even wind up a senator or governor before he's through."

"I don't care about any of that," Sylvia said.

"Exactly what did James write in his letter that upset you so?" Trent said.

"If you must know, he said he was very disappointed in the way I acted when he left, and that I still have some growing up to do," Sylvia said. "He said I should reflect on my behavior, and he hoped I used the time he was away to do some maturing."

Trent stared at his daughter. "And?" he said.

"What do you mean, *and*?" Sylvia said. "How dare he speak to me that way! Who does he think he is? He's nothing but a glorified cowboy."

"Sylvia," Trent said, and then sighed. "Never mind. Let's just finish our dinner."

"Eat all your supper or no dessert, and Mr. Dent baked a chocolate cake," Joey said.

"Yes, ma'am," Adam said.

"We need to go to town again tomorrow to see Mr. Cranston," Joey said. "I expect the both of you to be dressed and ready for breakfast by eight."

"Can I have my chocolate cake now, please?" Sarah said. "I finished all my supper."

"Let's go out to the porch where it's cooler, and we'll all have some," Joey said.

They went out to the porch. Mr. Dent brought out three slices of chocolate cake, two glasses of milk, and coffee for Joey.

"When is Jack coming?" Sarah said.

"I don't know," Joey said. "When his work is done, he'll let us know he's on the way."

"Jack is not afraid of anything, is he?" Adam said.

"I can think of one thing Jack is afraid of," Joey said.

"What's that?" Adam said.

"Me," Joey said.

"But you're a girl," Adam said. "And Jack is the biggest man I've ever seen."

"Girls are stronger than boys," Joey said.

"You're stronger than Jack?" Adam said.

"In a few years, what you'll come to understand is that you can't hit girls, can't understand girls, and that you can't live without them. That makes girls stronger than boys, Adam, and for that reason boys are afraid of girls."

"I don't understand," Adam said.

"Trust me, one day soon you will," Joey said.

Chapter Thirty

Cavill sat with his back against the saddle and smoked a cigar. Coffee was keeping hot over the fire and he drank a cup while he waited.

By his watch, it was noon.

Goodluck rode ahead right after breakfast and said he would return around noon or so, but there was no sign of him as yet.

Cavill spotted Duffy in the distance. He added some coffee to his cup and puffed on the cigar.

Fifteen minutes or so later, Duffy arrived and dismounted,

"I see you didn't hurry," Cavill said.

Duffy arched his back. "Where's Joseph?"

"Scouting up ahead," Cavill said.

"It looks like our Cherokee has turned southeast a bit," Duffy said as he grabbed a cup and filled it with coffee.

"At last signs, Goodluck put him at three days ahead of us," Cavill said.

Duffy sipped coffee and said, "He's slowing down."

"Goodluck seems to think he's already selected his next target and is just waiting on the next full moon," Cavill said.

"I had that same thought myself," Duffy said.

"Did you remember our cigars?" Cavill said.

"Got a box of twenty-four for both of you and forty pounds of supplies," Duffy said.

"Goodluck's coming," Cavill said.

"I got some fresh meat from town. How about a stew for lunch?" Duffy said.

"I found out something very interesting," Cranston said. "I wired the registry of deeds in Cheyenne and they replied that the ranch has already been sold."

"Sold? To who?" Joey said.

"A financial investment company in Arizona called Dunstable Incorporated," Cranston said. "It's located in Phoenix, and I can't seem to find much information on them other than it purchased the ranch a week after the parents were murdered."

"How could they buy it?" Joey said. "And who sold it?"

"The bank in Cheyenne held the mortgage to the land and was only too happy to sell it at cost just to be rid of it," Cranston said.

"I see," Joey said. "So they not only lose their parents, but they lose what little inheritance they might have gained from the ranch."

"They barely paid the mortgage and taxes on the land, Joey," Cranston said. "With them gone now, those children had no chance of hanging onto the ranch. It's better this way."

Joey nodded. "I understand," she said. "Thank you for trying."

"I tracked him to here before lunch," Goodluck said as he stopped his horse.

"Here is the middle of nowhere," Cavill said.

"We have three hours of daylight left," Duffy said. "Give the horses thirty minutes rest while I check the maps."

They dismounted and Duffy took out his maps.

"Goodluck, I think we're here, and those mountains in the distance are the Owl Creek Mountains," Duffy said. "And according to this map, they sit inside the Wind River Reservation."

"He's not going to the reservation," Goodluck said.

"I agree," Duffy said. "The full moon is in five nights. How far can he ride in five nights?"

"He's slowed his pace from forty to twenty-five miles a day," Goodluck said.

"So anywhere from a hundred and twenty-five to two hundred miles in any direction," Duffy said.

"If he's riding twenty-five, I say we ride forty and catch this son of a bitch before the next full moon," Cavill said.

Duffy looked at Goodluck and Goodluck nodded.

"That's what we'll do," Duffy said.

"This sitting around doing nothing is making me crazy," Porter said.

Porter and Miss Potts were in the lobby of the hotel after breakfast.

"Maybe we should return to the office," Miss Potts said.

"I just wish the men would report in and let us know where they are," Porter said.

"If they are near a telegraph, they would have," Miss Potts said.

"Did you wire the office for news? Maybe they have a telegram they haven't sent to us yet," Porter said.

"I did right after breakfast," Miss Potts said. "And again after lunch."

"Maybe the governor has some news," Porter said. "Let's take a walk over to his office and check."

Goodluck scouted ahead while Duffy built a fire and Cavill tended to Blue and Bull.

When the coffee was ready, Cavill filled two cups, sat next to

Duffy, and handed him a cup.

"This is it for me," Cavill said. "No more chasing outlaws halfway across the country. I've had enough."

"I have to say I agree with you, partner," Duffy said. "There is only so much of this kind of life a man can take."

"We have other considerations to think about," Cavill said. "Joey and Sylvia, my fighting and your law school. We're not getting that chasing some Cherokee outlaw through the mountains."

"You want to quit and go home?" Duffy said.

"You know better than that," Cavill said. "I want to catch this bastard and hang him from the first tree I come across."

"Here comes Goodluck," Duffy said.

Goodluck rode into camp and dismounted. "He's turned south directly into the mountains," he said.

"Can we catch him?" Duffy said.

"He's not in any hurry," Goodluck said. "Three days, maybe a bit more."

"See to your horse," Duffy said. "Feed him well. He's got to travel a long distance tomorrow."

Chapter Thirty-One

After breakfast, Joey took Adam and Sarah for a ride on the horses they selected for themselves.

Adam chose a medium-sized filly and Sarah a small bay. The children rode well, but that didn't surprise Joey as they were raised on a ranch.

Joey led them to the south range, where her cowboys were roping and branding young cattle.

"Let's get down and watch a while," Joey said.

They dismounted and stood near the cowboys.

"Adam, Sarah, there is something I need to tell you," Joey said.

They looked at her. "Yes," Adam said.

"You know that I spoke to Mr. Cranston yesterday in town," Joey said. "I asked him to find out about your ranch in Wyoming. He told me the bank sold it."

"Sold our ranch?" Adam said. "So we can never go back?"

"I'm afraid not," Joey said.

"So what happens to us?" Adam said.

"For now, you stay here with me," Joey said. "When Jack arrives, we can decide if you want to stay or go live with a relative somewhere."

"We don't have no relatives," Adam said. "All Sarah and me got now is each other."

"I wish Jack was here," Sarah said.

"Me too, honey," Joey said.

"Are you sending us away?" Sarah said.

Joey knelt beside Sarah and hugged her. "No, no, I'm not."

"I can ride and rope," Adam said. "Pa taught me. Brand, too."

"I believe you," Joey said. "Let's ride some more, you two owls."

"Owls?" Adam said.

"Nothing. Just something Mr. Cranston reminded me of," Joey said.

The three detectives rode twenty-five hard miles before stopping to rest the horses and prepare a hot lunch.

"I'm going to walk ahead for a bit and make sure we're headed in the right direction," Goodluck said.

"I'll take care of your horse," Cavill said.

While Duffy built a fire and put on some hot food, Cavill brushed the horses to cool them down. Only when they were cool enough did he give them water and some grain.

Duffy checked his maps as beans and bacon cooked in a pan. "We're headed straight to the Owl Creek Mountains on the reservation," he said.

"Goodluck seems sure he won't go there," Cavill said.

"I'd be surprised if he did, myself," Duffy said.

"Did you get some cornbread in town?" Cavill said.

"Two pounds and some biscuits," Duffy said.

"Cornbread goes better with beans," Cavill said.

"Joseph's on his way back," Duffy said.

When Goodluck returned, Duffy dished up three plates of food.

"This is not making any sense," Goodluck said. "I found his camp about a mile south of here. He barely rode ten miles from his last camp."

"He's biding his time, waiting on the full moon," Cavill said.

"It looks that way," Goodluck said.

"If that's true, he already has picked out his next victim," Duffy said.

"Where? On the reservation in the mountains?" Cavill said. "That doesn't make any sense."

"West of the mountains is a lot of prairie land," Duffy said. "There could be any number of ranches and farms for him to pick from."

"I say we ride hard until we catch him," Cavill said.

Duffy looked at Goodluck. "Is he headed for the mountains?"

"It certainly looks like it," Goodluck said.

"We got about seven hours of daylight left," Duffy said. "Let's make the most of them."

"Do you smell something?" Cavill said.

"Smoke," Duffy said.

"To the east," Goodluck said.

They rode east for about a mile to a hill. On top of the hill, they stopped and looked at the smoldering remains of a covered wagon below.

"Goddammit," Cavill said.

They rode down the hill and dismounted. A mother, father, and two children, a boy and a girl, lay around the overturned wagon, scalped and with their throats cut.

"These kids aren't more than ten and twelve years old," Cavill said.

Goodluck inspected the smoldering wagon. "Two days at most," he said.

Cavill pulled the folding shovel from his gear and extended it.

"I'll give you a hand," Goodluck said.

"I'll do it," Cavill said.

Duffy motioned to Goodluck to leave Cavill be and said,

"Let's check what we can for any information."

While Cavill dug a grave deep enough to house the entire family, Duffy and Cavill checked the unburned contents of the wagon.

They found identification that said the family was from Ohio and had recently purchased two hundred acres of land west of the mountains.

"He killed these people for fun," Duffy said. "It's still three days to the full moon."

"They just happened to be at the wrong place at the wrong time," Goodluck said.

"Scout ahead," Duffy said. "I'll wait here with Jack."

Porter and Miss Potts had lunch with Governor Hale in Hale's private quarters.

"Charles, I know we agreed it wouldn't do any good, but I have to do something," Hale said. "I'm authorizing the army to patrol every square mile in Wyoming to hunt this man. Maybe we'll get lucky before the next full moon."

"That train you use for personal use? Have it ready to travel at a moment's notice," Porter said. "Wherever he strikes, I want to be able to get there as soon as possible."

"I'll go with you along with a squad of marshals," Hale said.

"Miss Potts, you can return to the office if you'd like," Porter said.

"The hell I will," Miss Potts said. "I'm going on the train with you."

"Miss Potts, this is no place for a—" Porter said.

"If you say 'woman,' I'll hit you right in the head," Miss Potts said.

Porter sighed. "Governor?"

"Why not?" Hale said.

★ ★ ★ ★ ★

"We'll make camp on top of that ridge," Duffy said.

"We have an hour of daylight left," Cavill said.

"Jack, the horses have carried us sixty miles today," Duffy said. "They need rest and grain, or we'll be walking the rest of the way."

"All right," Cavill said.

They dismounted and, as Duffy built a fire, Cavill and Goodluck saw to the horses.

"I got a pound of fresh beef left, some potatoes and carrots, how about a beef stew?" Duffy said.

"Fine," Cavill said.

"We need water," Duffy said as he filled the coffee pot. "That stream we passed is just a few hundred yards away."

"I'll get it," Cavill said. He took the three canteens and headed to the stream.

While he was gone, Duffy got the stew going and made a pot of coffee.

"What's eating Jack?" Goodluck said.

"He gets this way sometimes when he takes a job personally," Duffy said.

"He's thinking of those kids," Goodluck said.

"Heaven help that Cherokee when we catch up to him," Duffy said. "Jack will kill him on sight."

"Can you stop him?" Goodluck said.

"Can you?" Duffy said.

Goodluck shook his head and started to laugh.

Chapter Thirty-Two

Halfway up the highest mountain in the Owl Creek Mountain Range, the three detectives dismounted and walked their horses to give them a break.

They walked until they reached a flat, grassy ridge.

"Where is this fool going?" Cavill said.

"The horses are played out," Duffy said. "We'll make camp here and give them a good rest."

"I'll scout on foot to make sure we haven't lost him," Goodluck said.

"Take your Winchester," Duffy said.

Goodluck grabbed his Winchester and set out on foot. He picked up the trail by searching for disturbed rocks and impressions left in the soft grass and earth.

He tracked for about a mile and was surprised to see an abandoned campsite that was just twenty-four-hours old.

Goodluck followed the tracks made by the Cherokee's powerful horse for about a half mile, until they turned and ascended a steep ridge.

Goodluck paused to look up at the very high peak of the mountain.

"He wants the higher ground," he said aloud.

Joey and Sarah stood outside the corral and watched as Adam worked with one of her hands inside the corral. Adam's father had taught the boy well. He knew how to rope and control a young colt.

Adam and the hand stood in the center of the corral after Adam roped the young colt, and together they had the colt trot in circles around them as part of the training process.

"Your brother knows what he's doing with a rope," Joey said.

"Pa and Adam used to rope all the time," Sarah said.

"Your pa was a good teacher," Joey said.

Joey placed her arm around Sarah, and the young girl hugged Joey around the waist.

"Come on, let's go inside and help Mr. Dent prepare supper," Joey said.

As they ate supper around a campfire, Duffy studied his maps. "This mountain must be nine thousand feet in elevation, maybe more. Where is he going?" he said.

"I do not think we are hunting him anymore," Goodluck said. "I think he is hunting us."

"That's why he wants the high ground?" Duffy said. "And why he slowed down."

Goodluck nodded. "Yes," he said.

"You think he's leading us into a trap?" Duffy said.

"I do," Goodluck said.

"Any ideas?" Duffy said.

"Scout ahead for a place where he can ambush us," Goodluck said. "Then look for a way around it and close his back door."

"And the horses?" Duffy said.

"We walk them as far as they can go," Goodluck said. "You follow from a distance while I look for a back door around him."

Duffy looked at Cavill. "Jack?"

"How sure are you he's setting a trap?" Cavill said.

"The high ground gives him a big advantage, and he's slowed his pace to allow us to fall into his trap," Goodluck said.

"The full moon is in two nights," Duffy said. "That means he'll look to trap us inside the next two days. Joseph, can we catch him before then?"

"I'll leave at dawn," Goodluck said. "I'll mark my trail. If I find a path around him, I'll wait for you to catch up before we proceed, but only if it's safe. No sense in the three of us getting killed."

Duffy and Cavill exchanged glances.

"Okay," Duffy said.

Porter and Miss Potts met Governor Hale for dinner at his private residence.

"I've dispatched the army and have secured the services of a dozen marshals," Hale said. "My train is prepared and ready to roll at a moment's notice."

"The full moon is in two nights," Porter said. "I guess we'll know in three."

Hale sighed heavily. "Wyoming can't afford another incident," he said. "I have reports of another dozen ranchers and farmers leaving the territory after the last incident. We'll never make statehood with this kind of violence hanging over our heads."

"Don't sell my people short, Governor," Porter said. "Just because they haven't sent word doesn't mean they aren't making progress."

Hale nodded. "I guess we'll know soon enough," he said.

Chapter Thirty-Three

Goodluck ascended slowly, making sure each step was sound and on the right track.

He guessed his elevation, by the thinner air and chilled winds, to be around seven thousand feet.

The thin air tired him, so he rested frequently. Besides his canteen and Winchester, Goodluck carried a small pouch of jerky and biscuits because he didn't want to be weighted down with heavier supplies.

He sat on a rock and ate a sliver of jerky and took a few sips of water.

The Cherokee wasn't far ahead, according to the tracks he left behind. No more than twelve hours at most.

As far as he could determine, this wasn't a good spot for an ambush. The slope was too pitched, the cover too protective, and he would need to expose himself in order to attack, leaving him open to a counterattack.

The Cherokee was experienced and smart.

Goodluck stood and continued to follow the tracks up the side of the mountain. One hundred fifty yards below, Duffy and Cavill followed with the horses in tow.

Despite the cool winds, Goodluck was moist with sweat. The terrain was harsh, and several times he nearly lost his footing and had to hug some rocks.

Although Goodluck believed the Cherokee to be evil and crazy, his respect for him grew with each misstep and gasp for air as he continued to climb.

There was a slight leveling of the mountain, and Goodluck sat in the shade and rested for ten minutes, taking a few sips of water.

When his legs felt a bit stronger, Goodluck stood and walked along the flat ridge, following the trail left behind by the Cherokee.

The ridge wound around the side of the mountain and opened up to a flat plateau of grass and trees.

Goodluck didn't like it. He paused and scanned the area for signs and then cocked the lever of his Winchester before proceeding.

He walked about a hundred yards and stopped beside a large clump of bushes. The mood struck him, and he began to pray silently.

Goodluck stopped in mid-prayer when he sensed something behind him, and he turned just as a rope was thrown around him.

The rope tightened, and Goodluck was thrown to the ground. He looked up at the Cherokee on his large horse.

When Duffy and Cavill reached the level ridge, Duffy said, "Jack, my horse has thrown a shoe."

"I don't like leaving Goodluck alone for so long," Cavill said.

"Go on ahead," Duffy said. "I'll catch up as soon as I put on a new shoe."

"Don't be long," Cavill said.

Holding Blue by the reins, Cavill started walking along the ridge, following Goodluck's tracks.

Goodluck was dragged behind the horse for several hundred yards, and then the horse stopped.

The rider dismounted with a second rope in hand. On one

end of the rope was a noose. He sat Goodluck on his horse and looped the noose around his neck.

"I know you, Joseph Goodluck," the Cherokee said.

"Go to hell," Goodluck said.

The rider returned to the saddle, tossed the end of the rope over a tree limb, caught it, kicked his horse, and Goodluck was lifted off the ground by his neck.

The ridge opened to a large, flat field of grass and trees.

Cavill spotted Goodluck's impressions in the grass and followed them. He led Blue about a hundred yards and then froze in place when he spotted Goodluck's Winchester rifle on the ground.

Deep impressions made from a large horse showed that Goodluck had been dragged away.

Cavill jumped into the saddle, cracked the reins, and followed the trail for another several hundred yards until he spotted Goodluck hanging from a tree limb.

"Goodluck," Cavill screamed and raced Blue across the field to the tree where Goodluck hung from a noose.

Cavill jumped to stand on the saddle, pulled his field knife, and grabbed the rope, slicing it in two. Goodluck dropped into Cavill's arms.

They fell to the ground. Cavill removed the noose, Goodluck coughed and spat, and Cavill rolled onto his back and said, "Jesus Christ."

Cavill sat up and grabbed his Colt and fired two shots in the air, replaced the Colt in the holster, and then stood and went for his canteen.

He splashed a bit of water on Goodluck's face and Goodluck opened his eyes and looked up at Cavill.

Goodluck tried to speak and Cavill said, "Don't talk, not yet."

Cavill turned when he heard Duffy's and Goodluck's horses approach.

"Jesus Christ, what happened?" Duffy said as he dismounted.

"I got here just in time," Cavill said.

Duffy looked at the noose on the ground. "Did you see him, Jack?" he said.

"No, but I'm going after him," Cavill said.

"Jack, he's to hell and gone by now," Duffy said.

"Stay here with Goodluck," Cavill said. He mounted Blue, tugged the reins, and raced toward the opposite end of the ridge.

Duffy knelt beside Goodluck. "Can you sit up?" he said.

Cavill followed the tracks to the edge of the ridge where they disappeared. He dismounted and tried to spot where the Cherokee had descended.

"Where did you go, you son of a bitch?" Cavill said as he looked for signs of disturbed rocks.

He walked the ridge for hundreds of yards, but it all seemed the same to him. Wherever the Cherokee had gone, it was impossible for him to tell.

Frustrated and angry, Cavill mounted Blue and raced back to Duffy and Goodluck.

Goodluck was sitting against his saddle, sipping water from a canteen.

Cavill slid off the saddle and said, "I need you to track him, Joseph."

"Jack, he's in no condition," Duffy said.

"He's getting away," Cavill shouted.

"Then he gets away," Duffy said.

"The hell he gets away," Cavill said. "Joseph, get up."

"Jack, would you just listen," Duffy said.

Goodluck motioned for Cavill to come closer. Cavill knelt

beside Goodluck.

"Sha-con-gah," Goodluck whispered.

"What?" Cavill said.

"Blueford Duck," Duffy said. "Also know as Blue Duck."

Cavill looked up at Duffy. "Son of a bitch," Cavill said.

"Let's make camp," Duffy said. "Come morning, we have some riding to do."

Chapter Thirty-Four

Miss Potts hurried from the telegraph office to the hotel with an urgent telegram for Porter.

She found Porter drinking coffee and smoking a cigar on the porch of the hotel. She handed him the telegram. "From Mr. Duffy," she said.

Porter read it quickly and stood up. "Let's go," he said.

"Where?"

"To see the governor," Porter said.

They walked quickly to Governor Hale's office at the capitol. He saw them in his office.

"This just came from my people," Porter said. "They're on the Wind River Reservation at Fort Washakie and request that you send your private train to pick them up."

Hale read the telegram. "I'll send my train immediately," he said.

Porter turned to Miss Potts. "Send the reply," he said.

Miss Potts nodded and dashed out of the office.

Porter took a chair. "The full moon was two days ago and there have been no reported killings," he said.

Hale nodded. "Charles, whatever you pay your people, it's not enough," he said.

Duffy and Cavill waited in Colonel West's office at Fort Washakie. West sat behind his desk, while Duffy sat in a chair and Cavill paced the room.

A soldier knocked on the office door.

"Enter," West said.

The soldier entered the office and handed a telegram to West.

West scanned the telegram and said, "Your train will be here by noon tomorrow."

"Thank you, Colonel," Duffy said.

"How is your man?" West said.

"I think we'll go find out," Duffy said.

"He has no broken bones or internal damage that I can detect," the doctor said. "I gave him some salve to put on the rope burns. Except for his voice being weak, he's in good shape."

"Where is he?" Duffy said.

"Taking a bath," the doctor said.

"Thanks."

They found Goodluck in the fort's bathhouse.

"Feel up to visiting the chief?" Duffy said.

Goodluck, Duffy, and Cavill dismounted at Chief Washakie's cabin.

The old chief was sitting in his rocking chair, smoking a cigar and drinking coffee.

"I did not expect to see you so soon," Washakie said.

"We need to catch the train in Green River and wanted to pay our respects," Duffy said.

"What happened to you, Joseph Goodluck?" Washakie said.

"I'll tell you over a cup of coffee," Goodluck said.

"Tell my grandson to fetch more coffee," Washakie said.

"The train is about to leave, Miss Potts," Porter said.

"Coming Mr. Porter," Miss Potts said.

Hale and Porter shook hands on the platform.

"I'll wire you as soon as possible," Porter said.

Miss Potts, dressed in pants and a blue dungaree shirt and boots, stood next to Porter.

"I've never seen you wear pants before, Miss Potts," Porter said.

"I just purchased them, Mr. Porter," Miss Potts said.

"Let's go then," Porter said.

Porter and Miss Potts entered the three-car train. A few moments later, it rolled away from the platform.

"Sha-con-gah," Washakie said. "Murdered his father, Buffalo Hump, when he was still a boy, believing it would make him a great war chief of all his people. Instead, it made him an outcast known as the outlaw Blue Duck."

Washakie's grandson filled cups with fresh coffee and passed them around.

Cavill lit a fresh cigar and gave it to Washakie, then lit one for himself.

"I find it strange that Blue Duck would be in Wyoming," Washakie said. "Arkansas, Texas, and Oklahoma are more to his liking."

"Chief Washakie, do you know where he would go to hide from the law?" Duffy said.

"He has a woman in the Indian Nation in Arkansas," Washakie said. "Her name is Belle Starr."

Chapter Thirty-Five

After breakfast with Washakie, Duffy, Cavill, and Goodluck rode south off the reservation toward Lander.

After a few hours, they reached the bustling oil well where workers, covered in the black smudge, were having a short break for coffee.

Farnsworth, seated on a wood box outside the mess tent, looked at Duffy, Cavill, and Goodluck as they dismounted.

"I remember you men," Farnsworth said. "You're the detectives."

"Spare a cup of coffee?" Duffy said.

Farnsworth stood up and said, "Come inside."

They entered the mess tent, where dozens of workers sat at tables with cups of coffee and slices of pie.

They grabbed cups at a table, filled them with coffee, and took an empty table.

"Mr. Farnsworth, we've identified the Cherokee Indian who attacked your men," Duffy said. "He's an outlaw named Blue Duck, sometimes called Blueford Duck. Ever hear of him before?"

"Can't say as I have, but I travel a lot, working on oil rigs," Farnsworth said. "Think he'll pass this way again?"

"Not likely," Duffy said. "By now he's probably gone into hiding. We're going to check on that now."

Farnsworth looked at Goodluck's neck. "What happened to you?" he said.

"We were tracking him through the Owl Creek Mountains," Goodluck said.

"And?" Farnsworth said.

"We caught up to him," Goodluck said.

"Thanks for the coffee," Duffy said.

"Still a shithole," Cavill said when they arrived in Green River.

They dismounted at the railroad depot. Across the wide, muddy street a small general store was open for business.

"We're early," Cavill said. "I'm going to see what that store has for cold drinks."

Cavill crossed the street and entered the store. A thin man wearing a white apron stood behind the counter.

"What do you have in the way of cold drinks?" Cavill said.

"Cold beer and sarsaparilla in bottles," the clerk said.

"I'll take three sarsaparillas," Cavill said.

"That will be thirty cents," the clerk said. "You get a penny for each bottle you return."

Cavill paid for the drinks and returned to Duffy and Cavill. They stood on the platform, sipped sarsaparilla, and waited for the train.

"Do you want anything at the general store?" Joey said as she parked the buggy outside the telegraph office.

"Can we get some candy?" Sarah said.

Joey stepped down from the buggy and then helped Sarah get down. Adam hopped out and stood next to Sarah.

Joey reached into a pocket of her work pants and gave Adam a dime. "Share what you buy," she said. "And Adam, hold your sister's hand."

"Yes, ma'am," Adam said.

"I'll meet you there as soon as I'm through here," Joey said.

Joey entered the telegraph office and sent a lengthy telegram to Cavill in care of his office. She wrote that Adam and Sarah were well, but that their ranch had been auctioned off by the government of Wyoming. She ended by asking him to write or telegraph as soon as possible.

The train arrived at twenty past twelve. The three detectives were very much surprised to see Porter and Miss Potts exit the riding car.

"Mr. Porter, what are you doing here?" Duffy said.

"I got antsy, waiting at the office for news," Porter said. "I was visiting Governor Hale when your telegram arrived requesting his train."

Cavill looked at Miss Potts. "I've never seen you wear pants before," he said.

Blushing, Miss Potts said, "They seemed appropriate for the trip."

"Get your horses stored away, we have a lot to talk about," Porter said.

As the train reached speeds of fifty-five miles an hour, Miss Potts served fresh coffee.

"He hung you, this bastard?" Porter said.

"If Jack hadn't come by when he did, I'd be dead and buried by now," Goodluck said.

"I had to save Joseph, or I'd a caught him for sure," Cavill said.

"I'm grateful you let him go," Goodluck said.

"How is your neck?" Porter said.

Goodluck moved his neckerchief and Miss Porter gasped at the sight of the rope burn.

"The doctor said I should keep putting the salve on the burn and the scar will fade with time," Goodluck said.

"Thank God you're alive," Porter said. "Now tell me about

this savage animal called Blue Duck."

"He's a stone-cold killer," Goodluck said. "But he usually kills only for gain or in a dispute. He likes Texas, Arkansas, and Oklahoma, so I can't figure out why he was in Wyoming Territory."

"He also has a woman he sometimes lives with, according to Chief Washakie," Duffy said. "Belle Starr."

"The Queen of Outlaws?" Porter said.

"If Blue Duck is hiding anywhere, he's with her in the Indian Nation in the Ozarks," Duffy said. "We figure to go there and find out."

"You'll need permission to enter the Indian Nation to serve warrants," Porter said.

"We figured," Duffy said.

"I'll go with you and see Federal Judge Parker to obtain the warrants," Porter said.

"The hell with all this nit-picking," Cavill said. "I'm going to find the bastard and hang him from a tree, just like he did to Goodluck, and leave him to rot."

"Mr. Cavill, you'll do no such thing," Porter said. "Or you can turn in your federal constable badge and resign your position this very moment."

"Not until after we catch him," Cavill said.

"We have to find him first," Duffy said.

"That won't be too difficult," Goodluck said. "Taking him is another matter."

"First things first," Porter said. "We need to go see Judge Parker in Fort Smith, Arkansas."

"At least we stopped the killings," Duffy said.

"Now we have to make him pay for them," Porter said and looked at Cavill. "Legally."

Chapter Thirty-Six

At the Doral Hotel in Wyoming, Duffy, Cavill, and Goodluck took hot baths after sending their dirty clothes to the hotel laundry.

"That rope burn is looking better," Cavill said from his tub.

"It feels better," Goodluck said. "But I'm almost out of the salve the doctor gave me. I'll have to get more."

There was a knock on the bathhouse door; it opened and Porter stepped in.

"We're having a late breakfast with the governor in thirty minutes," Porter said.

"There hasn't been one report from anywhere in Wyoming about a killing this past full moon," Hale said.

"That isn't entirely true, Governor," Duffy said. "While we were tracking him to the mountains, two days before the full moon, we came across a family of pilgrims moving to Wyoming and he murdered them. It appeared to be a chance encounter."

Hale nodded. "Nonetheless, it appears he's fled the territory," he said.

"We'll be leaving for Fort Smith in the morning to see Judge Parker," Porter said.

"This Blue Duck, what was his reasoning?" Hale said. "A man, any man, needs a reason to kill, what was his?"

"We don't know at this point, Governor," Duffy said. "But you can be sure we will find out."

"I'd like him to stand trial in Wyoming, if possible," Hale said.

"I'll ask Judge Parker about that," Porter said.

"By the way, where is Miss Potts?" Hale said.

"She had to run some errands," Porter said.

After purchasing tickets to Fort Smith at the railroad depot, Miss Potts stopped by Governor Hale's personal physician and picked up a jar of salve for Goodluck. Then she went to the telegraph office.

A telegram for Cavill was waiting to be picked up. It was sealed and marked *private*.

From the telegraph office, she returned to the hotel where Porter, Duffy, Cavill, and Goodluck were having coffee on the porch.

She handed the envelope with the tickets to Porter.

To Goodluck, she gave the salve.

To Cavill, she handed the telegram.

Opening the envelope, Porter said, "Miss Potts, there are five tickets in this envelope stamped Fort Smith."

"That's because I'm going with you," Miss Potts said.

"The hell you are. I need you at the office," Porter said.

"The office is fine, and you need me with you," Miss Potts said. "And that's the end of it."

Miss Potts stepped past Porter and entered the hotel.

Duffy, Cavill, and Duffy grinned at Porter. "Say it. Just say it," Porter said.

"Say what?" Cavill said.

"Never mind," Porter said. "So what do we know about this Blue Duck character that might be helpful?"

"He's Cherokee and highly skilled at tracking and riding," Goodluck said. "He's a big man like Jack and knows how to kill. We know he killed his own father, Buffalo Hump, to try and gain power. His attempt to gain power failed and made him an outcast."

"He lacks compunction," Duffy said. "Any man who kills the way he does without cause lacks a conscience."

"Do we know how he hooked up with Belle Starr?" Porter said.

"No, but according to Chief Washakie, they have a hideout in the Ozarks Indian Nation," Duffy said.

"I keep asking myself, what did he gain by murdering those people?" Porter said. "Even a man without compunction stands to gain from what he does, who he kills and when. This full-moon business—what does it all mean?"

"Fear," Duffy said. "We saw the fear in people's eyes at the approach of the full moon. They were terrified."

"Yes, but so what?" Porter said. "If all he wanted was to cause fear, he could have killed every night of the week. We discussed this before and decided nothing. He needs a reason to kill the way he does. What is that reason?"

"I'll ask him," Cavill said. "Right before he resists arrest."

Duffy and Goodluck grinned.

"Mr. Cavill, we discussed this before as well, and I won't tolerate—" Porter said.

"Tell Blue Duck that," Cavill said. "He's the one who hung Joseph."

Porter sighed. "Point taken," he said. "But I'd rather we took him alive so we can get answers to all these questions."

"What time does our train leave?" Cavill said.

"Ten tomorrow morning," Porter said.

"I'm tired of sitting around," Cavill said. "I think I'll go for a ride and stretch my legs."

After Cavill left, Porter looked at Duffy. "Keep him in check, Mr. Duffy," Porter said.

Duffy looked at Porter.

"At least do your best," Porter said.

Chapter Thirty-Seven

Cavill rode Blue ten miles south of Cheyenne, dismounted in a field, sat under a shady tree, and lit a cigar.

That's when he remembered Joey's telegram. He reached into his shirt pocket and tore open the envelope.

The news was disappointing about Adam and Sarah. A financial company called Dunstable Incorporated in Arizona had bought the mortgage on their parents' ranch. Joey said she had hoped to sell it and give the money to Adam and Sarah, but the mortgage was outstanding and taxes were due.

"They didn't waste any time, did they?" he said aloud.

Cavill tucked the telegram back into his shirt pocket and thought for a moment.

"No, they didn't," he said.

Standing, Cavill took the reins and mounted the saddle. "Let's go, boy," he said.

Duffy read the telegram and said, "Did you show this to Mr. Porter?"

"Not yet," Cavill said.

They were in Duffy's room. "He's in his room down the hall," Duffy said.

They walked down the hall and knocked on Porter's door. Porter opened the door. "Mr. Cavill, I see you're—"

"Read this," Duffy said.

"Come in," Porter said.

They entered the room and closed the door. Porter sat at the desk and read the telegram.

"It could be a coincidence that their ranch was purchased by this Dunstable Incorporated so soon after they were murdered, or it could be—" Duffy said.

"Planned," Porter said. "Find Miss Potts and Goodluck, and let's go see the governor."

"This Dunstable Incorporated, have they purchased the land of any other victims?" Hale said.

"We'd like to find that out," Porter said. "We need your help."

"Anything, Charles," Hale said.

"I'm leaving Miss Potts behind to research ranches and farms sold after the murders that took place during the full moon," Porter said. "This telegram could just be coincidence, or it could point to a devious plan. Either way, we need to know."

"What do you need me to do?" Hale said.

"Give Miss Potts total authority to research the Registry of Deeds and the banks," Porter said. "And assign her a few assistants from your staff."

"Anything to get to the bottom of this, Charles," Hale said.

"Good. I'll have Miss Potts report to you this afternoon," Porter said.

Cavill sent a telegram to Joey telling her he would be traveling to Fort Smith, hopefully to end the investigation. He also told her the information she sent about Adam and Sarah's ranch being bought by the Dunstable corporation might prove to be the key they had been hoping for to unlocking the whole mess.

After sending the telegram, Cavill joined the others for dinner at Hale's residence.

"Miss Potts has been assigned two of my top aides for as long as she needs them," Hale said. "I've sent a telegram to every bank in the territory to cooperate with my office and provide any information requested concerning ranches and farms sold during the year after a full-moon killing."

Porter looked at Miss Potts. "Miss Potts, there is no need for me to tell you how important this assignment is," he said.

"No need, Mr. Porter," Miss Potts said. "With the assistance of Governor Hale's office, I will get to the bottom of the matter."

"Good. Contact me through Judge Parker's office in Fort Smith, Arkansas, beginning tomorrow," Porter said.

After dinner, while Porter and Miss Potts stayed behind at Hale's office, Duffy, Cavill, and Goodluck had coffee on the porch of their hotel.

Cavill and Goodluck smoked cigars.

"Just what I fancy, another fourteen hours on a train," Cavill said.

"What I can't figure is how a man like Blue Duck fits into a company like Dunstable Incorporated," Duffy said. "If he fits at all. It could be just coincidence at this point that Dunstable bought the ranch so soon after Adam and Sarah's parents were murdered."

"Men like Blue Duck leave nothing to coincidence," Goodluck said. "If he was there, it was for a reason."

"You think he was paid to kill those people so Dunstable Incorporated could buy up the land?" Duffy said.

"Like you said before, men like Blue Duck need a reason for what they do," Goodluck said. "Money is a reason."

"What do you think, Jack?" Duffy said.

"I think I'm going to beat him to within an inch of his life," Cavill said.

"For what he's done, I think we'll let you," Duffy said.

Chapter Thirty-Eight

The train arrived in Fort Smith, Arkansas, a few minutes past noon. Duffy, Cavill, and Goodluck retrieved their horses from the boxcar and walked along the wide streets into town from the railroad depot.

"Must be five thousand people living here now," Porter said. "The first time I was here some twenty years ago, there were but a few hundred trying to make a town."

The hotel to which Porter sent a telegram was on Main Street facing the massive courthouse building dominating the town's landscape.

"We'll check in, stable the horses, and go see Judge Parker," Porter said.

Judge Isaac Parker was only in his mid-forties, but he appeared much older due to his long white hair and beard.

His reputation as "The Hanging Judge" was countrywide and well-founded. About ten years earlier, Parker sentenced eight men to die for their crimes; they were hanged on the same day, and his reputation was born.

"Twice I tried to hang that murderous son of a bitch, and twice he eluded me," Parker said. "If you men can bring him in alive, I'll sentence him to hang by the neck until dead. Our country is growing. There is no more room for outlaws like Blue Duck if we're to prosper as a society."

"We'll need warrants," Porter said.

"You'll need more than that," Parker said.

"I have some men. The best I employ. All are federal constables and first-rate lawmen," Porter said.

"Where are they?" Parker said.

Porter went to the door, opened it, and said, "Come in, men."

Duffy, Cavill, and Goodluck entered the office.

"James Duffy, Jack Cavill, and Joseph Goodluck," Porter said. "They have worked this investigation since the beginning."

"Governor Hale spoke very highly of you men in his telegram," Parker said. "However, I'd like to send Marshal Bass Reeves and maybe another marshal with you. Reeves lived with the Cherokee for several years and knows the people."

"We'd like to leave first light tomorrow," Porter said.

"They'll be ready," Parker said. "And if Belle Starr gives you any trouble, arrest her too."

"We'll see you in the morning to pick up the warrants and meet your men," Porter said.

"We'll need supplies for at least a week," Duffy said. "We can order them at the general store and pick them up in the morning."

"I'll need to rent a good horse," Porter said.

They were walking from the courthouse to their hotel when Duffy, Cavill, and Goodluck paused on the street.

"What?" Porter said.

"Mr. Porter, you're not going with us," Duffy said.

"And why not?" Porter said.

"Mr. Porter, this is a hard ride through the Ozarks and no place for a . . ." Duffy said.

"An old man?" Porter said.

"You haven't been in the saddle for a while, sir," Duffy said.

"I was riding ranges and chasing outlaws with cap and ball since before you were born, Mr. Duffy," Porter said. "A few mountains aren't going to dissuade me from joining you men."

"I saw some fine horses for rent at the stables where we boarded our horses," Goodluck said.

"Fine. Let's go take a look," Porter said.

They walked to the stables. Duffy and Cavill waited outside while Porter and Goodluck went in and took a look at the horses.

"What are we going to do, Jim?" Cavill said. "We can't have Mr. Porter slowing us down the whole trip."

"Mr. Porter is the boss," Duffy said. "And I doubt we can talk him out of coming with us."

"So, what do we do?" Cavill said.

"I don't know about you, but I'm going for a shave and a bath before dinner," Duffy said.

Cavill nodded. "Good idea," he said.

Porter and Goodluck emerged from the stables. "That horse will do just fine," Porter said. "Now, I need some proper trail clothes and a Winchester. Let's head to the general store, and I can get what I need when we order the supplies."

The hotel bathhouse had a Chinese, female barber, who was an expert with a razor and a pair of scissors.

While the water boiled for the bathtubs, she shaved Duffy and Cavill and gave each man a much-needed haircut.

When the tubs were ready, she added scented oils and bubble bath to the steaming hot water.

Cavill lit two cigars and gave one to Duffy.

As they soaked, they discussed what to do about Porter.

"Maybe we're selling him short," Duffy said. "He was . . ."

"Was," Cavill said. "He's what? Sixty-four now? That's a long way from *was.*"

"He might surprise us," Duffy said.

"Did I ever tell you I hate surprises?" Cavill said.

Goodluck entered the bathhouse. "There you are," he said.

"Mr. Porter said to tell you dinner is at six at the hotel."

"Joseph, what is your opinion of Mr. Porter going with us?" Duffy said.

"It's his money," Goodluck said.

"That's not an opinion," Duffy said.

"No, but it is a fact," Goodluck said.

"I've sent a telegram to Miss Potts for a report," Porter said. "As we'll be gone at least a week or more, I'd like to get some information before we leave."

"Maybe one of us should stay behind to communicate with Miss Potts?" Cavill said.

"Nice try, Mr. Cavill," Porter said. "Now let's order the best steaks in the house," Porter said. "It's been my experience that when going into the field, it's best to have a full stomach."

Chapter Thirty-Nine

Miss Potts sent a telegram to Porter in Fort Smith with a report on her findings. To date four ranchers and two farmers across Wyoming Territory had sold their property to the Dunstable Incorporated company for fractions of what the land was worth.

After sending the telegram, she returned to the office of the Registry of Deeds to continue her research.

The two aides provided by Governor Hale were already in the main hall, combing through recent transactions.

"We found two more ranches bought up by this company," one of the aides said.

"Keep looking," Miss Potts said. "I want a word with the governor."

As they were leaving the lobby of the hotel, a desk clerk said, "Mr. Porter, a telegram just arrived for you."

Porter read the telegram quickly and said, "Miss Potts has made some progress. She's uncovered four ranches and two farms recently bought by Dunstable Incorporated."

"It can't be coincidence," Duffy said.

"It never is, Mr. Duffy," Porter said. "Let's get our horses and supplies."

"Mr. Porter, this is Marshal Bass Reeves and Marshal Frank Cochran, two of my best deputies," Judge Parker said.

Reeves, a stout black man, had been born a slave in Texas.

During the war, he ran away and lived with the Cherokee in Oklahoma. Cochran, Irish, was an experienced lawman with a reputation for being fearless.

Cochran looked at Porter. "If you don't mind, sir, you look a little past it for a trip like this."

"I don't mind a bit, sonny," Porter said. "Judge, thank you for the warrant."

"Good luck, men," Parker said. "And remember, I want that bastard to stand trial and hang legally."

"Governor Hale, it's become quite obvious this Dunstable Incorporated is buying up land in Wyoming Territory with some kind of inside help," Miss Potts said. "It can't be coincidence that the moment a property goes up for sale, they are there to buy it."

"I agree," Hale said. "What do you propose?"

"I'd like to go to Phoenix, where they are registered," Miss Potts said.

"Alone? I'm afraid Mr. Porter wouldn't approve of me allowing you to do that."

"Then have your aides accompany me," Miss Potts said.

"I can't allow that, Miss Potts," Hale said. "If something were to happen to you, Charles would never forgive me."

"I do not need your permission to purchase a train ticket, Governor," Miss Potts said.

"No, you don't," Hale said. "Still, Charles wouldn't approve."

"If he were here, we'd go together, but he's not," Miss Potts said.

"I'll assign two US Marshals to escort you to Phoenix," Hale said. "Find out what you can find out, and then come right back to Cheyenne."

"Yes, Governor," Miss Potts said. "And I'll report back to you later this afternoon on our findings."

"Marshal Reeves, take us to the Cherokee Nation," Porter said.

The citizens of Fort Smith didn't know what was happening, but they always stopped to watch a team of marshals ride away from the courthouse along Main Street.

"Three days' ride into the mountains," Reeves said. "And I'm glad Mr. Goodluck is with us."

"Why is that?" Porter said.

"He increases our chances of not getting scalped," Reeves said.

Miss Potts returned to the Registry of Deeds and spent the afternoon doing research with the two aides.

She was astounded to discover eleven small ranches and five farms had been purchased by Dunstable Incorporated.

"That's it for today," Miss Potts said. "I need to get my train ticket, pack my bags, and see the governor."

Miss Potts walked to the railroad depot and purchased a round-trip ticket to Phoenix on a train scheduled to leave at ten the next morning. From there she returned to the hotel to pack and change and then went to see the governor.

Hale insisted she have dinner with him, along with the two marshals who would be escorting her to Phoenix.

"Sixteen properties purchased by this Dunstable Incorporated," Hale said. "And no one has questioned this before now?"

"Every transaction is legal and certified by the bank," Miss Potts said. "What is suspicious to me is how this company in Arizona has been able to react so quickly to people selling their property in Wyoming."

"That is puzzling," Hale said.

"Excuse me, ma'am, but exactly what are we going to

Phoenix for?" one of the marshals said.

"Miss Potts is going to check into the Dunstable company, and you are entrusted with her safety," Hale said. "And nothing had better happen to her. Not even a cold. Is that clear?"

"Yes, Governor," one of the marshals said.

"Good," Hale said. "Now let's have some coffee and dessert."

Chapter Forty

Led by Reeves, the group of detectives, along with Charles Porter, traveled a hard forty miles before dark.

Cavill and Duffy kept an eye on Porter during the ride, but he appeared to take it in stride.

They built a fire and tended to the horses while a supper of beef stew cooked in a large pot.

They ate with their backs against their saddles.

"Marshal Reeves, do you know where Belle Starr has her hideout in the mountains?" Porter said.

"No, but you can bet the Cherokee people do," Reeves said. "That's why we're going to talk to them first."

"You lived with them," Duffy said. "What was that like?"

"I wasn't a slave," Reeves said. "To them I was a whole man, a free man. That's what it was like."

Duffy nodded. "Could you have stayed? After the war, I mean?"

"I did stay," Reeves said. "For two years. But I wanted to make a life of my own, and they understood. I became a farmer and got married."

"How did you become a marshal?" Duffy said.

"I was a terrible farmer," Reeves said. "When Judge Parker took over the court about ten years ago, I applied as a deputy marshal and he appointed me. I've been with him since. The judge knew I lived with the Cherokee. The reservation is his jurisdiction, he knew I spoke the language, and I became his liaison between the reservation and the judge. So to speak."

"His reputation as the Hanging Judge, is it warranted?" Duffy said.

"When he was appointed by President Grant, Fort Smith was a lawless place," Reeves said. "Full of murderers, cutthroats, rapists, and worse. He established law and order, not only by hanging those who deserved it, but by doing it swiftly in the public square. Those looking to commit crimes decided it was better to do it outside of the judge's jurisdiction."

Reeves stood up. "Best build up the fire for the night. It gets cold up here in the Ozarks this time of year."

"I'll give you a hand," Cavill said.

Despite the high speed of the train, Miss Potts slept comfortably in her sleeping car, woke refreshed, and, after washing and changing, met the two marshals in the dining car for breakfast.

If the train kept to schedule, they would arrive in Phoenix by eight o'clock that night.

"Miss Potts, do you know what Phoenix is?" one of the marshals said.

"A town," Miss Potts said.

"It's a wild place. I had to pick up a prisoner there about a year ago," the marshal said. "Because of the railroad, it's a trade center with twenty saloons, a half-dozen dance halls, and a dozen brothels. It's not safe for a single woman to walk the streets day or night."

"But I'm not single," Miss Potts said. "I have you two capable marshals to protect me. Day or night."

"Yes, ma'am," the marshal said.

After breakfast, Miss Potts returned to her private car and worked on her notes.

She read each page carefully several times. Each transaction from the Dunstable Incorporated company came from the First

Bank of Phoenix in the form of a bank draft sent from the bank in Phoenix to the banks holding the mortgages in Wyoming. Signatures and names were never required with a bank draft, so the person behind the purchases at Dunstable remained a mystery.

A mystery she hoped to solve in Phoenix.

After breakfast, Reeves guided the other men through twenty miles of passes and high ground through the Ozark Mountains.

They broke at one for an hour to eat a cold lunch and rest the horses.

"I must say these mountains are a desolate place, Marshal Reeves," Porter said.

"To you they might appear so, but Cherokee scouts have had eyes on us for half the day now," Reeves said.

Porter and the others looked around at the vast hills and mountains.

"Why don't they show themselves?" Porter said.

"They will, when we get close enough and they have reason to," Reeves said.

When the horses were rested, they rode another twenty miles before dark.

"Make camp," Reeves said. "I want to scout ahead."

"I'll go with you," Goodluck said.

Reeves and Goodluck rode ahead for several miles. Reeves pointed to a narrow pass between two mountains. "We'll cross that clearing tomorrow," he said. "We'll be in the Indian Nation once we clear that pass."

"How long to reach the reservation from there?" Goodluck said.

"Late afternoon."

"I saw some wild turkeys a few hundred yards back," Goodluck said. "I think I can pick off a couple for supper."

"You fire a gun, and the Cherokee scouts will want to know why," Reeves said.

"Who said anything about a gun," Goodluck said.

They backtracked to the field where twenty or so turkeys pecked away at the ground. Goodluck removed his bow and two arrows from his gear, and from a distance of four hundred feet, he took down two birds.

"Quite a feast you provided, Mr. Goodluck," Porter said as they carved into the golden brown turkeys that had been roasting on open spits.

"Nature provided the feast. I provided the arrows," Goodluck said.

"Tomorrow we'll be on reservation land," Reeves said. "We'll be greeted by Cherokee scouts and escorted to the center of the settlement. You'll see that most wear the cross of Christianity, but make no mistake about it. These are warriors through and through, so watch your step at all times. And whatever you do, insult nobody."

"We'll take great care and watch our step," Porter said.

"I'll do the talking until you are addressed," Reeves said. "Chief Red Fox and most of the others speak English and many speak French and Spanish, but Red Fox will speak English first."

"Is there anything else we need to know?" Porter said.

"What day is tomorrow?" Reeves said.

"Saturday," Porter said.

"I can tell you one thing for sure. We'll all be going to church on Sunday," Reeves said.

Chapter Forty-One

The train arrived in Phoenix a few minutes early. When Miss Potts and the two marshals stepped onto the platform, they were greeted with the sound of piano music and laughter.

"From the saloons and dance halls, ma'am," one of the marshals said.

Off in the distance, a gunshot sounded.

"Do either of you gentlemen know where our hotel is located?" Miss Potts said.

"Yes, ma'am," a marshal said. "It's a piece."

"A little walk never hurt anybody," Miss Potts said.

"Yes, ma'am," the marshal said.

Joey, Adam, and Sarah had dessert on the porch so they could watch the setting sun. Joey had coffee with her pie. Adam and Sarah had glasses of milk.

"Miss Joey, are we going to live here with you, or are you going to send us to a home when Jack gets back?" Adam said.

"If Jack wanted to send you to a home, he wouldn't have sent you here to me," Joey said.

"I want to stay here with you," Sarah said. "I don't want to go to a home."

"If you stay with me, there will be certain rules you have to follow," Joey said. "You'll have to go to school when it's in session, and you'll each have chores to do every day."

"We both went to school and did chores back home," Adam said.

"Then we have an agreement?" Joey said.

"Yes, ma'am," Adam said.

"Yes, Miss Joey," Sarah said.

Joey extended her right hand. "Shake on it," she said. "And then maybe we can have another piece of pie."

Fortunately, the hotel was located on a side street away from the noise of the loud saloons and dance halls.

The walk through town was unsettling, as they passed saloon after saloon where cowboys hung around in the streets with glasses of beer and whiskey bottles.

Thankfully, most of them weren't armed.

After checking into her room, Miss Potts and the marshals had a late supper in the hotel restaurant.

"Tomorrow morning we will start at the First Bank of Phoenix, where all the bank drafts originated," Miss Potts said. "They must have records of where Dunstable Incorporated is located and who owns it or controls it."

"Yes, ma'am," a marshal said.

"The banks open at nine, so we'll meet for breakfast at seven-thirty," Miss Potts said. "And please find the telegraph office. I'd like to send a telegram to Governor Hale and see if they found additional land purchases."

"Yes, ma'am," a marshal said.

"And for God's sake, please stop calling me *ma'am,*" Miss Potts said. "You may call me Miss Potts."

"Yes, ma'am," a marshal said.

"Well, goodnight then, gentlemen," Miss Potts said.

"Miss Potts?" a marshal said.

"Yes."

"Tomorrow is Saturday," the marshal said. "The banks aren't open."

"Oh. I see. I guess we'll see the mayor and speak to the town sheriff," Miss Potts said. "Somebody must know something about Dunstable Incorporated."

"Yes, ma'am."

Chapter Forty-Two

By noon, Reeves led the group through the pass that led to the reservation land. He stopped the group and scanned the prairie, hills, and mountains.

"Is there a problem, Marshal Reeves?" Porter said.

"Ride single-file behind me," Reeves said.

Reeves continued riding, and the other men fell in line behind him. At the end of the pass, Reeves and the group found themselves suddenly surrounded by twenty Cherokee warriors armed with Winchester rifles.

"Nobody move. Nobody speak," Reeves said.

Reeves broke away from the group and rode slowly to the leader of the Cherokee warriors.

"Good to see you again, Rajan," Reeves said in English. "It's been too long. How is Red Fox these days?"

"The chief is well," Rajan said. "Who are your people?"

"Lawmen like myself," Reeves said. "We have come to speak with Red Fox and seek his help."

Rajan nodded. "Come," he said.

Reeves followed the Cherokee warriors as Rajan rode beside him. Behind them, Porter and the others followed closely.

They rode for about two hours and finally arrived at the center of the reservation. Most of the Cherokee lived in cabins. There was a wood schoolhouse, a brick church, shops, and a medical facility.

Riding to the reservation, they passed fields of corn and wheat and tobacco.

At the largest cabin, Rajan dismounted. "I shall see if my uncle is awake," he said. "He takes many naps these days."

Rajan entered the cabin and returned in a few moments and said, "Reeves, who speaks for the lawmen?"

"Mr. Porter," Reeves said.

"You and Porter, come in," Rajan said.

Reeves and Porter dismounted. They walked up to the porch; Rajan held the door open for them and then he followed them inside.

Chief Red Fox sat at a wooden table in the kitchen. He was a handsome man of about seventy. He wore a blue shirt, dark pants, and boots. A silver chain with a crucifix hung around his neck.

"Bass, it's been too long, my old friend," Red Fox said.

"I am pleased to see you, Chief," Reeves said.

"Sit. Rajan, bring us coffee," Red Fox said.

Reeves and Porter sat at the table, and Rajan brought three cups of coffee.

"And your friend is?" Red Fox said.

"Charles Porter. A powerful lawman," Reeves said.

Red Fox looked at Porter. "Charles Porter, you have come here for a reason," he said.

"Yes, to ask for your help," Porter said.

"Ask," Red Fox said.

"My men and I seek to capture the outlaw Blue Duck," Porter said. "We believe he is hiding out in the mountains with the outlaw Belle Starr."

Red Fox nodded as he stuffed an old, well-worn pipe with tobacco from a pouch. "Blue Duck is a very dishonorable man," he said.

"Yes, but do you know where he might be hiding with Belle Starr?" Porter said.

Red Fox turned to Rajan and spoke to him in Cherokee. Rajan nodded and replied in Cherokee.

"Rajan will escort you with twenty warriors to see Belle Starr," Red Fox said.

Porter looked at Rajan. "Thank you," he said.

"Thanks are not needed," Red Fox said. "We do not like Blue Duck."

"When can we leave?" Porter said. "We are most anxious to capture him."

"Tomorrow you attend church as my guest," Red Fox said. "Leave early Monday. Tonight, you sit at my table for supper in the hall."

"Thank you, Chief Red Fox," Porter said.

"Bass, you can share my cabin tonight," Red Fox said. "Rajan, show Mr. Porter and his people to our guest cabins."

"Ma'am, I am elected to keep vigilance over this town, not engage in its banking practices," Sheriff Bregman said.

"I am not disputing your duties, Sheriff," Miss Potts said. "But the marshals and I have come a very long way to gain information about the Dunstable Incorporated company."

"I appreciate what you're saying, but I have no knowledge of such a company or who runs it," Bregman said. "That would be the bank's department."

"What about complaints?" Miss Potts said. "If someone filed a complaint against them, wouldn't it go through you?"

"It would if there were any," Bregman said.

"Thank you for your time, Sheriff," Miss Potts said. "Where may I find the mayor?"

"Try his office," Bregman said.

Mayor J.T. Cole owned the largest saloon in Phoenix, as well as a dance hall that also served as a brothel.

Cole met Miss Potts and the marshals in his office above the saloon.

"A fine company, Dunstable Incorporated," Cole said. "Has done a lot to help commerce in Phoenix grow."

"Such as?" Miss Potts said.

"Well, I'd have to consult with the town council and chamber of commerce to get all the facts," Cole said.

Miss Potts stared at Cole for a moment. "Mayor Cole, you have no idea what I'm talking about, do you?" she said.

"Umm, well, no," Cole said. "However, if you—"

"Thank you for your time, Mayor Cole," Miss Potts said.

"This is a nice cabin," Cavill said as he, Duffy, and Goodluck settled their gear on three beds.

Porter and Cochran shared a second cabin closer to Chief Red Fox.

"We have time for a shave and a bath," Cavill said.

Duffy opened the back door and stepped onto the back porch. "Jack, Goodluck, come here," he said.

Cavill and Goodluck joined Duffy.

"Have a look," Duffy said.

Cavill and Goodluck looked at the small hut attached to the cabin.

"What is that?" Cavill said.

"See that rain barrel on the roof?" Duffy said. "That copper tube?"

"Yeah," Cavill said.

"That's an outdoor shower with the water heated by the sun," Duffy said.

"Like a fancy hotel," Cavill said.

"It's a modern world," Goodluck said.

★ ★ ★ ★ ★

Miss Potts and the two marshals had dinner at the hotel dining room.

"Don't you find it a bit odd that a company that has dispatched so much business in Phoenix seems to be unknown to the sheriff and mayor?" Miss Potts said.

"The sheriff spends most of his time breaking up bar fights and arresting drunks," a marshal said. "And the mayor runs a saloon and a whore . . . I mean brothel. I wouldn't put too much stock in their knowledge."

"Can you gentlemen do a favor for me?" Miss Potts said.

"If possible," a marshal said.

"Can you find out where the bank president lives? Perhaps we can speak with him before Monday," Miss Potts said.

"We'll look into it right after dessert," a marshal said.

Most people on the reservation ate in their cabins. The great hall was reserved for special occasions. The hall held one hundred people, and every table was occupied.

Porter and the group sat at Red Fox's table.

Before a dozen women served a dinner comprised of several types of beef dishes, Red Fox introduced Porter to the priest who would hold Mass on Sunday, and the reservation doctor, a man named Scott.

Scott was a white doctor from back east, something that was unheard of only ten years earlier, when only black doctors were allowed to practice on reservations. Scott not only relished the idea, he volunteered for the job.

Red Fox and Reeves chatted like father and son during the meal. Porter and the rest of the group were mostly silent unless asked a question.

After supper, Red Fox insisted coffee be served at his cabin, and the group followed him home.

Rajan made and served the coffee. Red Fox smoked his pipe. Cavill, Goodluck, and Porter smoked cigars.

"Now I ask a question," Red Fox said. "You told me you were after Blue Duck, but did not say why. So I ask: why?"

"Since the month of January, Blue Duck has been killing farmers and ranchers in Wyoming during the full moon. We don't know his reason for doing this, but he has to pay for his crimes."

"It is unlike Blue Duck to allow himself to be seen," Red Fox said. "He's a skilled tracker, hunter, and warrior, and he knows how to use the night to his advantage."

"He left a witness alive he thought he killed," Porter said. He turned to Goodluck and nodded.

Goodluck opened a button on his shirt. "We were tracking him through the mountains," he said. "He backtracked, took me by surprise, and gave me this."

Goodluck revealed the ugly rope burn on his neck.

"Jack Cavill and James Duffy were nearby and saved my life," Goodluck said.

"So Blue Duck doesn't know you're alive?" Red Fox said.

"No, he doesn't," Goodluck said.

"When I was in Washington, DC, a few years ago to discuss a treaty, I read a book that was in French," Red Fox said. "It was called *The Art of War,* by a great Chinese chief."

The bank president's name was Varnell, and he was highly annoyed at being disturbed at home while having dinner with his family.

"Miss Potts, I am having a quiet evening at home with my family," Varnell said. "Whatever your business is with the bank, it can wait until Monday morning. Now goodnight."

"Mr. Varnell, you may have noticed that these two gentlemen are wearing the badges of United States Federal Marshals,"

Miss Potts said.

"Yes, yes, what of it?" Varnell said.

"You can talk to us now, or on Monday morning they will present you with a warrant, and we will shut your bank down, confiscate all your records, and take our sweet time about it," Miss Potts said. "It's up to you how and when we talk."

"Can they really do what you said?" Varnell asked.

"I assure you they can," Miss Potts said. "Do you wish to talk here or at the bank?"

"The bank," Varnell said.

"What was he talking about back there?" Cavill said. "With *The Art of War,* I mean?"

"Strategy," Duffy said. "I think what he means is, since we don't know what we're walking in to, we need to plan carefully how we take Blue Duck."

"I have an idea about that," Goodluck said.

"Let's hear it," Duffy said.

"After I think about it some more," Goodluck said.

Sheriff Bregman knocked on the door of the bank when, as he was making his rounds, he saw lights on in the office.

One of the marshals opened the door.

"Can I help you, Sheriff?" the marshal said.

"Oh, it's you," Bregman said. "Is Mr. Varnell with you?"

"Unless you think we're robbing the bank," the marshal said.

"I'm here, Sheriff," Varnell said. "We're conducting an audit."

"Okay then. Goodnight," Bregman said.

After Bregman left, Varnell said, "Now what in God's name do you people want?"

"You have an account here in the name of Dunstable Incorporated," Miss Potts said.

"We do. What about it?" Varnell said.

"We're investigating a series of murders that have taken place in Wyoming over the past nine months during the full moon," Miss Potts said. "Are you aware of this situation?"

"Yes," Varnell said. "Even in so far away a place as Phoenix, we do get newspapers. What does that have to do with me and my bank?"

"The Dunstable Incorporated company, after each murder, has purchased property from people leaving Wyoming," Miss Potts said. "What we'd like to know is how this company receives its news so quickly and manages to buy up the land before anybody else."

"I'm sure I don't know the answer to that," Varnell said.

"This is your bank, and Dunstable Incorporated is your client," Miss Potts said.

Varnell sighed. "It is and they are, but I am not responsible for how they spend their own money," he said.

"But you are responsible for the transactions that come through your bank?" Miss Potts said.

"Yes."

"Can you tell us when the account was opened, how transactions are conducted, and where Dunstable Incorporated is located?" Miss Potts said.

"If it will make you go away," Varnell said.

Varnell went to his desk, sat, and used a key to unlock a large drawer. He removed a large ledger book, opened it, and flipped through the pages.

"Here it is," he said. "Now, what would you like to know?"

"When was the account opened and by whom?" Miss Potts said.

"Eleven months ago by a Mr. J. Frazier from back east. Philadelphia to be exact," Varnell said. "His orders were to purchase, through bank drafts, land that became available, upon his request."

"How does that work exactly?" Miss Potts said.

"I receive a wire from Mr. Frazier about a piece of property he wants to purchase, and I wire the funds to the receiving bank. It's all perfectly legal, I assure you," Varnell said.

"Maybe so, but didn't you question the fact that all the purchases are in Wyoming?" Miss Potts said.

"Why would I question that?" Varnell said. "If Mr. Frazier wants to spend his own money on buying land in Wyoming, it is none of my business."

"What does Mr. Frazier look like?" Miss Potts said.

"I only saw him one time when he opened the account," Varnell said. "He was around fifty or fifty-five, tall and slender-like. Had thick, graying hair and beard. He was soft-spoken and what I would describe as a gentleman. Is there anything else?"

"How much did he open the account with?" Miss Potts said.

"One hundred and fifty thousand dollars in cash."

"How much is left?" Miss Potts said.

Varnell scanned the ledger book. "Seventy thousand."

"Mr. Varnell, if you are again contacted by Mr. Frazier about buying additional land, send me a telegram immediately to Cheyenne, in care of Governor Hale," Miss Potts said. "If you fail to do so, the marshals will be paying you another visit, so it would be wise to do as I ask."

"As I have broken no laws and don't plan on breaking any, I shall wire you in Cheyenne if Mr. Frazier contacts me again," Varnell said. "May I return to my dinner now?"

"Goodnight, Mr. Varnell," Miss Potts said.

Chapter Forty-Three

After Sunday Mass, Reeves spoke to Chief Red Fox about the urgency of leaving to find Blue Duck.

Red Fox consulted with his nephew Rajan, who agreed with Reeves.

"Gather your warriors and leave after breakfast," Red Fox said.

Breakfast was served in the great hall, although only Red Fox, Porter and his group, and Rajan and his warriors attended.

By eleven in the morning, Rajan led the way on the three-day ride to Belle Starr's secret hideaway on the Oklahoma side of the Ozark Mountains.

Miss Potts and the marshals caught the noon train back to Cheyenne.

She spent the afternoon in her sleeper car making notes.

At six o'clock, Miss Potts met the marshals for dinner in the dining car.

"After we reach Cheyenne and report to Governor Hale, I'm afraid we must go to Philadelphia," she said.

"Why, ma'am?" a marshal said.

"To find Mr. Frazier, of course," Miss Potts said.

"Yes, ma'am," the marshal said.

Rajan brought enough supplies to feed a small army, carried on a riderless horse.

As supper cooked in a dozen pots and fry pans, Duffy and Cavill filled cups with coffee and went for a short walk.

"What do you think about the old man?" Cavill said.

"He's held up," Duffy said.

"It hasn't been rough yet, and there's been no shooting," Cavill said.

"Mr. Porter is no stranger to shooting," Duffy said. "Twenty years ago he—"

"That was twenty years ago," Cavill said. "He sits at a desk now, and that doesn't help the reflexes any."

"What are you suggesting?" Duffy said.

"Watch him close," Cavill said. "One of us stays with him at all times, especially if there's shooting."

"Agreed," Duffy said. "Let's get back before we're missed."

"Why do we need to go to Philadelphia?" a marshal said. "Ma'am. Can't we wire the marshals to—"

"You heard Mr. Varnell. This J. Frazier person is from Philadelphia. His corporation has to be registered somewhere," Miss Potts said. "And I'd rather go myself than leave it in uncertain hands."

"Philadelphia is a large and dangerous city, ma'am," a marshal said.

"Not if you have two marshals to protect you," Miss Potts said.

Both marshals sighed. "Yes, ma'am," one of them said.

After supper, Goodluck told stories of the old days forty years ago when many of the territories were still ruled by the tribes. Texas had just become a state, but most white men never strayed north of the Canadian River, for the great warriors such as Buffalo Hump ruled the land.

Bass Reeves told stories about being a slave on the Reeves

Plantation in Arkansas before the war.

"When the war broke out, Mr. Reeves went to fight for the South and, as many did, he brought a few slaves with him," Reeves said. "I was born a slave, but I was determined not to die one. A few days before the Battle of Wilson's Creek, I hit old George Reeves on the head during a card game, run off to the Indian Nation, and lived with the Cherokee People until the war ended."

"What did you do after the war?" Porter said.

"Became a farmer near the town of Van Buren and married Nellie Jennie out of Texas," Reeves said. "I farmed for about ten years until Judge Parker asked me to be a marshal in his court. I been doing that ever since, mostly because I'm a better marshal than I was a farmer."

Rajan was born on the reservation and knew no other way of life other than what he was born into.

"My father and grandfather would tell stories about the olden days before the reservation life," Rajan said. "My people ran free through Arkansas, Oklahoma, Texas, and Missouri. When I was a boy, the elders would tell stories of the great Trail of Tears and the shame they felt as a people."

"It was not what I would call our finest hour," Porter said.

"Judge Parker once told me when he asked me to become a marshal that all the things good and bad that happen are what make a country stronger. He said that after the war, the country rebuilt itself and became a stronger nation because of it. He told me that all the bad in my life made me a better, stronger person. I tend to believe him, because I'm here to talk about it," Reeves said.

"A wise man, that judge," Porter said.

"I'm going to do something wise right now," Reeves said. "I'm going to get some sleep."

Chapter Forty-Four

Miss Potts took the time to type her report to Governor Hale on one of the typewriters in the secretarial pool at his office before meeting with him.

"Who is this J. Frazier?" Hale said after he read the report.

"Apparently, he's the president of Dunstable Incorporated and the man who writes the checks," Miss Potts said.

"Yes, but who is he? What do we know about him?" Hale said.

"Nothing," Miss Potts said. "Which is why I must go to Philadelphia."

"Go to . . . Why?" Hale said.

"Dunstable Incorporated is registered there, and Frazier identified himself as being from there," Miss Potts said. "So there must be some records on file about who he is and where he lives and all that."

"Mr. Porter would—" Hale said.

"Do the exact same thing," Miss Potts said.

"Philadelphia is a large and dangerous city, Miss Potts," Hale said.

"Not if you're traveling with two marshals," Miss Potts said.

Hale sighed. "I suppose not," he said.

"Have there been any additional murders reported since my trip to Phoenix?" Miss Potts said.

"No," Hale said. "Apparently driving Blue Duck out of Wyoming has put an end to the killings."

"Have they found any additional land purchases by Dunstable?" Miss Potts said.

"No, they have not."

"The two are definitely related, Governor," Miss Potts said. "The marshals and I will be on the next train to Philadelphia."

"Should I notify anyone that you're coming?" Hale said.

"Heavens, no," Miss Potts said. "The last thing we want to do is give whoever is behind this horror advance warning."

Hale nodded. "Miss Potts, do be careful," he said. "The last thing I want to do is get Charles Porter's ire hot."

The trek into the mountains proved slow going. Several times Rajan, Reeves, and Goodluck scouted ahead while the others rested their horses.

By nightfall they had covered close to twenty-five miles of hard mountain country that was rough on the horses and rough on their backs.

After dark, the temperature dropped twenty degrees, so they built several fires for cooking and warmth.

"Another night, and by midday the next morning we will be at Belle Starr's secret cabin," Rajan said.

"Your people don't like Blue Duck, do they?" Porter said.

"The stories about him are true," Rajan said. "He has evil in his heart and his spirit. He has broken every white man's law as well as the laws of the Cherokee."

"Why is he allowed to roam free in the mountains?" Porter said.

"Blue Duck is also smart enough to know to stay off the reservation land," Rajan said. "They call the Ozark Mountains the Indian Nation, but that is only true of the reservation, and not the western mountains where Belle Starr has made her camp."

"If he is with Belle Starr, we will bring him to justice and make him pay for his crimes, rest assured on that," Porter said.

Miss Potts and the two marshals boarded an eastbound train for Philadelphia at ten p.m. The seventeen-hundred-mile trip would take thirty-four hours to complete, and had a scheduled arrival time of eight in the morning.

The dining car opened at nine, and Miss Potts and the marshals had a late supper before going to their sleeper cars.

After retiring to her car, Miss Potts was unable to sleep, so she worked on her notes for a while.

It wasn't the excitement of visiting a large city that kept her awake. She had been to Chicago, San Francisco, Boston, and New York on various assignments in the past.

It was the idea that, for the first time ever, she was working on her own as an agent. That's what got her blood pumping and her mind racing. She wasn't wishing Duffy and Cavill well as they rode off, or following Mr. Porter around like a puppy dog. No. For the first time in a dozen years, she was on her own.

And proving her value to the agency.

She studied her notes until her eyes grew heavy and then settled in for the night.

Goodluck and Reeves went off to hunt game while Rajan led the rest of the group to Belle Starr's hideout.

Goodluck and Reeves tracked the prints of a large mule deer for about a half mile until Goodluck motioned to stop.

They dismounted, and Goodluck removed his bow and six arrows from his gear. Reeves took his Winchester rifle. Goodluck led the way up the side of a steep hill.

The trail led from the steep hill to rocky, low mountains until Goodluck spotted the deer about one hundred and fifty yards to the right, on a cliff.

Goodluck placed an arrow into the string and took careful aim. The arrow traveled silently to the mark, and the deer fell dead from a neck wound.

They climbed to the deer and Goodluck used his field knife to remove the gut sack. Then he placed the animal across his shoulders.

When they returned to their horses, Goodluck tied the deer across the back of his saddle, then he and Reeves rode hard to catch up with the group.

Rajan stopped the group in a clearing about a hundred yards from a mountain stream to rest the horses and allow Goodluck and Reeves to catch up.

Duffy and Cavill and several of Rajan's warriors carried canteens to the stream to fill them with water.

"The old man is looking tired," Cavill said.

"So are the rest of us," Duffy said. "It's this country. It will wear you down quick."

"Nothing a hot bath, warm bed, and a steak wouldn't fix," Cavill said.

"That's going to have to wait," Duffy said.

"Yeah."

By the time they filled all the canteens and returned to camp, Goodluck and Reeves had come back.

"You wanted a steak. Joseph brought you one," Duffy said.

"Let it bleed out the rest of the day," Goodluck said. "Tonight I'll carve it up."

As they ate a light lunch, Duffy broke out his maps and studied the area. "Rajan, where are we?" he said.

Rajan looked at the map and pointed.

"And Belle Starr is where?" Duffy said.

Rajan traced his finger to a spot on the map. "Here," he said.

"Forty miles," Duffy said. "We'll be there by noon tomorrow, like Rajan said."

As he lit a cigar, Cavill said, "Joseph, I think it's time you told us of your plan."

Chapter Forty-Five

Joey and Sarah stood at the corral and watched Adam and her foreman rope horses. For a boy of twelve, Adam could rope and control a horse nearly as well as her foreman.

"Sarah, go in the house and put on a dress," Joey said. "We're going to town this morning."

"Yes, ma'am," Sarah said.

"And brush your hair," Joey said. "I don't want you looking like a wild animal."

Sarah nodded and ran to the house.

"Adam, five minutes, and you come out and change," Joey said. "We're going to town."

The train was thirty minutes late in arriving at Philadelphia, and Miss Potts and the marshals didn't step onto the platform until eight-thirty.

As she and the marshals walked from the platform to the streets, the first thing to strike Miss Potts about Philadelphia was how bad the air smelled. It was a mixture of stale water off the Delaware River, factories, oil-filled smoke, and horse manure.

"Good grief, do you gentlemen smell that?" she said.

"Yes, ma'am," a marshal said.

"We've smelled worse," the other marshal said. "Chicago, Boston, and especially New York City smell worse."

"Let's find our hotel and figure out where to go first," Miss Potts said.

"We'll need to take a horse taxi, ma'am," a marshal said. "I'm afraid it's too far to walk."

The marshals hailed a taxi. Miss Potts was surprised at how wide and busy the downtown streets of Philadelphia were. Carriages and wagons were everywhere, and people were scurrying like frightened rabbits.

Sanitation men wheeled large drums through the streets, picking up horse droppings.

Police in uniforms directed traffic at nearly every corner.

Telegraph polls lined the streets, and she noticed that many of the lines went directly to certain buildings.

"The telegraph is very popular in this city," Miss Potts said. "Some even have it in their homes."

"No, ma'am," a marshal said. "Those lines going to homes and buildings are for the telephone."

"Telephone?" Miss Potts said. "I need to get out of Springfield more."

"Yes, ma'am," a marshal said.

At the post office, Joey gave Adam and Sarah a dime each and told them she would meet them at the general store.

"Tell Mr. Finch I'll be along directly," Joey said.

"Yes, ma'am," Adam said.

As Adam and Sarah turned, Joey said, "Adam, take your sister's hand."

Adam took Sarah's hand, and they walked to the general store.

Joey entered the post office for the mail. It was the usual stack, minus a letter from Cavill.

Next Joey went to the feed and grain to order supplies for the next month. After that, she visited the blacksmith's shop and ordered one hundred pairs of new shoes.

After leaving the feed and grain store, Joey walked to the general store. Adam and Sarah were sitting in chairs out front, eating licorice sticks.

"Is that what you bought?" Joey said.

"Yes, ma'am," Adam said. "A penny apiece."

"Good. You can save one for me," Joey said. "Let's go back in. I need a few things."

Joey bought some yarn, needles, work gloves, and canning jars. When she looked around, she said, "Adam, where is your sister?"

"Looking at dolls," Adam said.

"I see," Joey said. "Wait here with Mr. Finch."

Joey went to the section of the store that carried toys and dolls and found Sarah looking at a porcelain doll from Germany.

"You like her?" Joey said.

"Yes, ma'am. She's beautiful," Sarah said.

"If I get it for you, do you promise to take very good care of her?" Joey said.

"Oh, yes, ma'am," Sarah said. "I promise."

The look on Sarah's face all but melted Joey, and she said, "Very well, take her to the counter."

Sarah scooped the doll up into her arms and they went to the counter.

"Mr. Finch," Joey said. "The boy needs a rifle. What do you have that's suitable for a twelve-year-old?"

"Winchester makes a fine youth model," Finch said.

"Let me see it," Joey said.

Finch removed a Winchester 73, made especially for youths, from under the counter and handed it to Joey. "Adam, can you handle a rifle like this?" she said.

"Yes, ma'am," Adam said. "I went hunting with Pa lots of

times, and could handle his Winchester and sometimes the Henry."

"Okay then," Joey said. "Mr. Finch, we'll take the rifle and the doll and a box of ammunition."

Miss Potts and the marshals took a taxi from the hotel to the Philadelphia Chamber of Commerce.

It was a large office building, four stories high, and Miss Potts and the marshals were shuffled from office to office before finally being directed to the membership director, Mr. Lohan.

"How may I help you, Miss Potts?" Lohan said after she and the marshals were escorted into his office.

"We are seeking information on a company called Dunstable Incorporated that is supposedly based here in Philadelphia," Miss Potts said.

"I take it by the two marshals escorting you that your inquiry is not of a friendly nature," Lohan said.

"If you could check your records, I'd appreciate it," Miss Potts said.

Lohan stood up from his desk, turned to the large bookcase behind him, and removed a thick ledger book marked with the letter D.

"What was that name again?" he said.

"Dunstable Incorporated," Miss Potts said.

Lohan flipped pages in the ledger book, going back and forth several times. "I am sorry, but I have no record of any such business," he said.

"Are you sure?" Miss Potts said.

"I am positive," Lohan said. "Not every business in the city chooses to join the Chamber of Commerce, although I can't imagine why one would choose not to."

"What about pending applications?" Miss Potts said.

Lohan sighed and then replaced the book. "There must be a

thousand applications waiting to be processed," he said.

"Well, there are four of us," Miss Potts said.

"You aren't going to go away, are you?" Lohan said.

"No," Miss Potts said.

Lohan sighed again. "Very well," he said.

Among the four of them, it only took about an hour to scan the thousand applications. Dunstable Incorporated was not in the pile.

"May I offer a suggestion?" Lohan said.

"Yes," Miss Potts said.

"If this company is incorporated, it would have to be on file as a corporation," Lohan said. "Try the Pennsylvania Corporations Office. If it's on record, that's where it will be."

"Thank you, Mr. Lohan," Miss Potts said. "And where can I find that office?"

"Two blocks south of here," Lohan said.

"Can you recommend a nice place for lunch?" Miss Potts said.

Chapter Forty-Six

Goodluck, Cavill, Duffy, and Rajan scouted ahead while Porter and the rest stayed hidden behind a steep hill about one mile west of Belle Starr's cabin.

The cabin was nestled against another steep hill and afforded protection from the rear. A corral sat in front with a small barn to the right.

Two horses were in the corral. One of the horses was as large as Cavill's.

The detectives and Rajan watched from a hill about three hundred yards away. Goodluck used binoculars to zoom in on the large horse.

"I only saw the horse for a few seconds, but I believe it's the same horse," he said.

"Smoke from the chimney," Duffy said. "So someone is home."

"Goodluck, what do you say?" Cavill said.

"We need to be sure Blue Duck is in that cabin," Goodluck said.

"I agree," Duffy said.

"Tie our horses out of sight, and Joseph and I will scout out the house," Cavill said. "We'll report back when we're sure."

"We should move back another half mile so we can make a cook fire undetected," Rajan said.

They rode another half mile to the west and made camp.

"Mr. Duffy, if they have not returned by dark, ride back and check on them," Porter said.

"I'll go with you," Rajan said.

While the horses rested, the group built several fires and Rajan made deer meat stew while Duffy heated some baked beans.

A bit later, as the group ate, using their saddles as backrests, Porter said, "I pray Blue Duck is in that cabin. I'd hate to think we wasted so much valuable time."

"Even if he isn't, Belle Starr will know where he is," Duffy said.

"I'm getting too old for this kind of waiting," Porter said.

"Why don't I get an update," Duffy said as he grabbed a small pot with a cover and filled it with stew and beans. "Bass, hand me a hunk of bread."

Cavill and Goodluck watched as Belle Starr came out of the cabin to use the outhouse located next to the barn.

She was quick doing her business and, as she returned to the cabin, she grabbed a few logs from the woodbin on the front porch.

"Be dark in a few hours," Cavill said. "Once they light a few lanterns, we should be able to see who else is inside."

"Someone is coming," Goodluck said.

"Yeah, I hear it, too," Cavill said.

Duffy walked up the side of the hill and set the pot and bread between Goodluck and Cavill.

"The old man is getting antsy for information," Duffy said.

"So far we've seen Belle Starr when she went to use the outhouse," Cavill said.

"Any sign of Blue Duck?" Duffy said.

"Not yet," Cavill said.

Goodluck removed the lid from the pot. Duffy took out two

spoons from his shirt pocket and gave one each to Cavill and Goodluck.

"Goodluck tasted the stew. "Who did the cooking?"

"Rajan made the stew," Duffy said.

"He knows how to cook," Goodluck said.

Cavill tried a spoonful. "Could use a little salt," he said.

"I knew you'd say that," Duffy said and took the saltshaker out of his shirt pocket and handed it to Cavill.

"The door is opening," Goodluck said.

The door to the cabin opened, and Blue Duck stepped out onto the porch. He held a bottle of whiskey in his right hand and took a swallow from the bottle before placing it on the porch railing.

Then he opened his pants and urinated off the porch.

When he finished, he buttoned up his pants, grabbed the whiskey bottle, and went back inside the cabin.

"That was him," Goodluck said. "That was Blue Duck."

"I'll go back and tell Porter," Duffy said.

"Tell him we're staying until they go to sleep," Goodluck said.

"Why?" Duffy said.

"So I can disable their horses," Goodluck said.

"What does this Blue Duck look like?" Porter said.

"He's a big man," Duffy said. "Not as big as Jack, but close. Black hair to his shoulders. Wore a dark leather vest over a red shirt."

"Marshal Reeves, Cochran, can either of you identify Blue Duck by sight?" Porter said.

"Never had the pleasure," Cochran said.

"Me neither," Reeves said.

"Rajan?" Porter said.

"I have seen him from a distance," Rajan said. "Enough to

recognize him."

"We'll wait for Mr. Cavill and Goodluck to return before we turn in," Porter said.

Cavill and Goodluck kept vigilant watch over the cabin until around ten o'clock at night, when the cabin door opened and Blue Duck drunkenly stumbled out to relieve himself again.

When Blue Duck stumbled back inside and closed the door, the lanterns went out a few minutes later.

"Give it an hour just to be sure," Goodluck said. "Blue Duck may be passed out drunk, but we don't know about Belle Starr."

An hour later, Goodluck removed his boots and, guided by the sliver of moon in the night sky, he made his way down to the corral.

He entered the corral slowly and quietly approached Blue Duck's large horse. The horse didn't mind and barely moved as Goodluck stroked and patted his neck.

When the horse was comfortable enough, Goodluck used his field knife to remove all four horseshoes.

Then he did the same for Belle Starr's horse.

"You're one crazy son of a bitch, you know that?" Cavill said when Goodluck returned and put his boots on.

Goodluck grinned. "Let's go back and get some sleep," he said.

Chapter Forty-Seven

Miss Potts felt slightly discouraged as she settled in her hotel bed for the night.

The Pennsylvania Corporations Office had no record of Dunstable Incorporated on file anywhere in the state.

An official named Mr. Ross was very nice about the lack of information and offered some kindly advice.

"If a company calls itself a corporation without registering itself with a corporations office and the Internal Revenue Service, chances are it's a fake," Ross said. "The west is littered with them, I'm afraid. Snake-oil salesmen selling miracle cures for every ailment known to man. When they get caught or arrested, they simply change their names."

"Can someone legally call themselves a corporation and operate as one without registering with a corporations office and the Internal Revenue Service?" Miss Potts said.

"No, they cannot," Ross said.

"He uses the name J. Frazier from Philadelphia," Miss Potts said. "Is it possible he has registered other corporations under that name?"

"It's possible. Unlikely, but possible," Ross said.

"Can you check?" Miss Potts said.

Ross sighed. "Come back in the morning," he said.

She had hoped for something more substantial than "Come

back in the morning," but she wasn't ready to give up just yet.

Somebody somewhere had to know J. Frazier.

Duffy, Cavill, Porter, Reeves, and Cochran rode over the hill at sunrise and stopped thirty feet in front of Belle Starr's cabin.

"Belle Starr and Blueford Duck, we have a warrant for your arrest," Porter shouted from atop his horse.

They waited thirty seconds and then Porter shouted, "Blue Duck, we know you are in there. It's useless to hide or try to escape. Come out now, or we will burn the cabin and force you out."

The door slowly opened and Belle Starr poked her head out. "I ain't wanted for a damn thing," she said.

"True enough," Porter said. "But Blue Duck is. Now stand aside, or we'll burn the cabin. Blue Duck, you have ten seconds to show yourself."

Belle Starr exited the cabin with a mug of coffee and took a chair.

"Come on out, Blue Duck," Porter said.

Blue Duck, dressed in dark pants, red shirt, and black vest, walked out onto the porch. He had a cup of coffee in his hand.

"What do you want, law dog?" Blue Duck said. "You are disturbing my breakfast."

"We are here to arrest you and to take you back to Judge Parker's court in Fort Smith," Porter said.

"For what?" Blue Duck said.

"A dozen counts of murder in the Territory of Wyoming, for starters," Porter said.

Blue Duck took the chair next to Belle Starr. "I never been to Wyoming Territory," he said.

"We say otherwise," Porter said. "Now come down off that porch."

"Do you have any witnesses?" Blue Duck said. "I have killed

men, women, and children from Texas to Canada, and nobody has ever even had a good look at my face before today. You can take your warrant and wipe your backside with it, for all I care."

Porter sighed and then held up his right hand.

Rajan, Goodluck, and the twenty warriors rode over the hill and stopped behind Porter.

Goodluck removed his neckerchief and stared at Blue Duck.

"Do you remember me?" Goodluck said.

Blue Duck stood up and looked at Goodluck.

"You should remember the faces of the men you hang," Goodluck said.

"So you see, we do have a witness," Porter said. "And all we need is one."

"Cowards, the lot of you," Blue Duck said.

"Enough talk," Cavill said.

Cavill dismounted and walked to the porch. Without saying another word, he walked up the steps to Blue Duck and punched him in the face with so much force that Blue Duck shattered the porch railing as he fell to the ground.

Cavill jumped down, grabbed Blue Duck, and yanked him to his feet. "Hang my friend, will you," Cavill said and punched Blue Duck again.

Blue Duck hit the ground again and reached inside his boot for a knife.

Cavill stepped on Blue Duck's hand and then yanked him up again and pummeled him with punch after punch until Blue Duck was but a limp rag doll.

"Mr. Duffy, you'd best stop him before there is nothing left to bring back," Porter said.

Duffy rode his horse to Cavill and gave Cavill a gentle nudge. "Jack, that's enough," he said.

Cavill released Blue Duck, and Blue Duck fell to the ground.

Porter turned to Goodluck. "Is Mr. Cavill always so . . . ?"

"Always," Goodluck said.

"Let me know when he fights again, so I can bet on him," Porter said.

"I have no corporation registered to a J. Frazier anywhere in the state of Pennsylvania," Ross said.

"Is there any way I can find out if J. Frazier is a resident of Pennsylvania?" Miss Potts said.

"You can try the Department of Census," Ross said. "If this Frazier lives in Pennsylvania, it would be on record with them."

"Where can I find the Department of Census?" Miss Ross said.

"Harrisburg," Ross said.

Miss Potts sighed. "Thank you," she said.

"Judge Parker told me to leave you be unless you interfered with the arrest of Blue Duck, so I see no reason to bring you along," Porter said.

Seated in her chair, Belle Starr sipped coffee from a mug and smoked a cigar. She looked at Porter. "You ain't seen the last of Blue Duck yet," she said.

"Good day," Porter said.

He left the porch and walked to the corral where Goodluck was shoeing Blue Duck's horse.

"Ready?" Porter said.

"Yes," Goodluck said and led the horse out of the corral.

Blue Duck waited beside Cavill and Duffy. Blue Duck was in his stocking feet. Cavill handed him the reins. "Since you like to spend so much time without your boots, you can ride without them," he said.

Blue Duck grinned at Goodluck. "Squaw," Blue Duck said.

"When they hang you, no one will be there to save you," Goodluck said.

Porter turned to Rajan. "Tell your chief what we did here," he said.

"That will have to wait," Rajan said. "We will go with you to Fort Smith so the whites can see that the Cherokee people are no friend to Blue Duck."

Porter looked at Blue Duck. "We won't tie your hands, but make no mistake, if you run, we will shoot you down."

Porter turned to Rajan again. "Take us to Fort Smith," he said.

For the third time in a week, Miss Potts and the marshals found themselves on a train. Luckily, the ride from Philadelphia to Harrisburg was a mere four hours.

She and the marshals enjoyed a nice breakfast one hour after the train left the station, then relaxed in the riding car until they arrived in Harrisburg at noon.

They took a taxi to City Hall, where the census department was located.

The first stop was to see the mayor. There the marshals explained that they were conducting a federal investigation and needed information on J. Frazier, who claimed to be from Philadelphia.

The mayor escorted them to the records division and told the clerks to assist the marshals and Miss Potts with whatever information they needed.

Two clerks checked census records for the name Frazier. The search took several hours to conduct.

Miss Potts and the marshals went to lunch at a small restaurant a block from City Hall.

When they returned, the clerks were just about finished searching the letter F.

"I'm afraid you aren't going to like the results," a clerk said. "We kept the search to people named Frazier who have the first name J, and we found more than three thousand residents statewide."

"Three thousand?" Miss Potts said.

"It would have been ten times that number had we searched for just the last name Frazier," a clerk said. "After all, Pennsylvania has more than four million residents."

"Does the census list information about employment?" Miss Potts said.

"Not employment as in where they work, but what their profession is," a clerk said.

"I suppose the marshals and I can do a cross-reference," Miss Potts said.

"That would take you at least three days," a clerk said.

"I'd best send a wire to the governor in Wyoming," Miss Potts said.

"You can use our telegraph," a clerk said.

After supper, Cavill tied Blue Duck's hands and legs with rope.

"I hear one word out of you tonight, and I'll finish what I started," Cavill said.

"I like big men like you," Blue Duck said. "They make more noise when I kill them."

"You want me to gag you?" Cavill said.

"Just remember what I said," Blue Duck said.

Cavill joined the group around the campfire.

"We will stand watch over him all night," Rajan said.

"We'll do our share," Cavill said.

Rajan nodded.

"How long to Fort Smith?" Porter said.

"Two days' ride from here," Rajan said.

"Mr. Porter, we have Blue Duck, but we still have no idea why he did what he did," Duffy said. "Don't you think we should question him?"

"I can tell you right now that son of a bitch won't tell us a thing," Porter said. "But he might talk to the judge."

Chapter Forty-Eight

"Miss Potts, we are just wasting our time here," one of the marshals said. "There is no connection between any of these men named Frazier and the Frazier in Phoenix."

"If you ask me, whoever the man is in Phoenix, he just made the name up out of thin air," the second marshal said.

They were at a large table in a conference room at City Hall.

"One thing Mr. Porter has taught me is that there is no such thing as coincidence," Miss Potts said. "Mr. Porter uses science, forensics, and investigation to solve a crime, and make no mistake about it, what we are investigating is a crime of the highest order."

"What's forensics?" a marshal said.

Miss Potts sighed. "You gentlemen have lived in the wilderness too long," she said.

"Exactly what are we looking for, ma'am?" a marshal said.

"A connection between the Dunstable Incorporated company in Phoenix and J. Frazier in Philadelphia," Miss Potts said.

"Ma'am, here is a J. Frazier in a place called Dunstable Township," a marshal said.

"Let me see that," Miss Potts said.

She took the document and read it quickly. "J. Frazier lives in Dunstable Township," she said. She looked at the marshals. "Coincidence?"

"I suppose that's where we're going next?" a marshal said.

"You suppose correctly, Marshal," Miss Potts said.

As they rode along a winding path through the Ozark Mountains, the sudden sound of gunshots halted the group.

"Everybody stay put," Duffy said. "Jack, Goodluck, let's check it out."

They followed the sound of shots to a ridge about two hundred yards to the west and dismounted. Getting down on their stomachs, they peered over the edge of the ridge.

Three men on higher ground had one man pinned down behind a large boulder.

"Come on, Marshal, what are you waiting for?" one of the three men shouted.

"Marshal?" Duffy said. "Joseph, ride back for Marshal Reeves. We need to see if he knows this man."

Goodluck mounted his horse and raced back to the group.

"You men, I'll see you hang in Judge Parker's court," the marshal shouted.

"I guess you'll be walking us back then, seeing as how we kilt your horse," one of the three men shouted.

"I'm going to give you one chance to surrender," the marshal shouted.

"He has grit. I'll give him that," Cavill said.

"No horse and three guns won't beat grit, Jack," Duffy said.

Goodluck returned with Reeves, and they got down beside Duffy and Cavill.

"That's Cal Witson," Reeves said. "I know, because he wears an eyepatch over his left eye from a wound during the war. What's he doing here?"

"About to get killed," Duffy said.

"Maybe we should help him out?" Cavill said.

"Hang on, Cal! We'll get you out of there," Reeves shouted.

"Who all is up there?" Witson shouted.

"It's me, Bass," Reeves shouted. "Who's shooting at you?"

"Banjo brothers," Witson said.

"Banjo brothers," Reeves said. "They're wanted for every crime there is in Arkansas. We best get Cal out of there."

"They have good cover," Cavill said. "Get your Winchesters and keep them busy while Jim and I come up behind them."

Reeves and Goodluck grabbed their Winchesters and fired at the Banjo brothers while Cavill and Duffy found a good place to scale down the ridge.

Porter and Cochran suddenly appeared and joined in with their Winchesters.

"Who all is down there?" Cochran said.

"Cal," Reeves said.

"Cal? What's he doing here?" Cochran said.

"I'll ask him as soon as we get him out," Reeves said.

Below, Cavill and Duffy made their way behind the Banjo brothers.

"Are those my men?" Porter said.

"Sure are," Reeves said.

"Keep firing. Give them a chance to get behind those three," Porter said.

With no choice but to keep their heads down, it was easy for Cavill and Duffy to sneak up behind the Banjo brothers.

Duffy waved for the shooting to stop.

"You three are surrounded," Duffy said. "Throw down your guns and come out."

One of the Banjo brothers spun around to shoot Duffy and Cavill shot him twice in the chest.

"Anybody else want to try my friend?" Duffy said.

"Your men got some hard bark on them, Mr. Porter," Reeves said.

★ ★ ★ ★ ★

Miss Potts and the marshals found lodging at a boardinghouse for the night. Supper was an extra fifty cents on top of the two dollars for a room.

As they ate supper, Miss Potts said, "According to the train schedule, we can get a train to Williamsport in the morning and then rent a buggy and ride to Dunstable Township."

"We need to send a wire to Governor Hale and let him know we'll be here for several more days," a marshal said.

"Two, maybe three days, at most," Miss Potts said.

"What you said before about coincidence. This is no coincidence, is it?" a marshal said.

"Hardly," Miss Potts said.

"What are you doing out here, Cal?" Reeves said.

"The judge got antsy for information and sent me to see Chief Red Fox," Witson said. "The Banjo brothers rushed me and chased me into that canyon. Shot my horse out from under me. Lucky you came along when you did. I don't know how long I could have held them off."

The two remaining Banjo brothers were on the ground, tied with rope.

"You mean you wasn't after us?" one of the Banjo brothers said.

"I didn't even know you were in these parts," Witson said.

"Our brother got kilt for no reason," a Banjo brother said.

"You brother got killed because he was a fool," Cavill said.

"All right, let's mount up. We're losing daylight," Porter said.

"We don't ride with no stinking Indians," a Banjo brother said.

"Then we'll tie a rope around you, and you can walk," Porter said.

CHAPTER FORTY-NINE

"Where do you think you're going?" Trent said to Sylvia as she entered the living room wearing a formal evening dress.

"To the cotillion in town, Father," Sylvia said.

"Should you be doing that?" Trent said. "You are spoken for, Sylvia."

"By a man who has been gone a month or more," Sylvia said. "And besides, I don't think he's ever coming back at all."

"Sylvia, James Duffy is as fine a—" Trent said.

"Don't start with that again, Daddy," Sylvia said. "I am not going to miss the biggest cotillion of the year because James Duffy is off somewhere playing detective."

"Who is escorting you?" Trent said.

"Bob Creed."

"Robert Creed is a fine young man," Trent said. "I'd like a word with him when he arrives."

"Very well," Sylvia said. "I need to finish my hair."

While Sylvia was in her room, Robert Creed knocked on the door. Trent went to let him in.

"Hello, Robert. It's been a while," Trent said.

"Yes, sir," Robert said.

"How are your folks?"

"Just fine, sir."

"Robert, I don't need to tell you this, but I will anyway," Trent said. "Sylvia is spoken for by a fine man named James Duffy. He is away on business at the moment, so I expect you to act like a proper gentleman. Understood?"

"I understand, sir," Robert said. "And don't worry."

"I'll see if Sylvia is ready," Trent said.

"Tomorrow we'll be in Fort Smith," Porter said to Blue Duck. "You can help your case considerably by talking to me before you see Judge Parker."

"What case?" Blue Duck said. "You have no proof I killed anybody, and your witness is alive. Even if he claims I tried to kill him, I didn't succeed, so all the judge can charge me with is attempted murder."

"I see you know our laws," Porter said.

"I know a lot of things," Blue Duck said.

"We'll see what you know when you stand before the judge," Porter said.

"How about some food?" Blue Duck said. "I'm hungry."

Porter turned and went to the campfire where several pots and pans of food were cooking.

"He wants some food," Porter said.

"I'll get it," Goodluck said.

He filled a plate with stew and bread and brought it to Blue Duck. Blue Duck's hands were free, but he was tied around the waist to a tree, as were the Banjo brothers.

Goodluck handed the plate to Blue Duck.

"Squaw," Blue Duck said.

Goodluck squatted in front of Blue Duck.

"When they hang you, I will request to be the hangman," Goodluck said.

"They won't hang me," Blue Duck said. "And when I am free, I will hunt you down like the squaw you are and finish what I started."

"They'll hang you, and when they do, I will make sure the rope is not tied properly so that you don't die right away,"

Goodluck said. "You'll hang there for a very long time, choking to death and waiting for the end. You'll soil your pants like a baby, and I will watch and smile as you die."

Blue Duck glared at Goodluck.

Goodluck stood and returned to the fire.

"What did Blue Duck say?" Porter said.

"He'd like some salt," Goodluck said.

Miles City closed Main Street for the annual cotillion. Tables with food and drink were set up on both sides of the street. An elevated platform had been built for a band to play on. More than five hundred people attended the event.

The center of the street had been kept clear for couples to dance in, and Sylvia danced a dozen dances with various partners as Robert watched from the sidewalk.

A man Robert didn't recognize took Sylvia to the punch bowl, and they each drank a glass. Robert rushed to her side.

"Sylvia, your father—" Robert said.

"Isn't here and I am having fun," Sylvia said.

Another man approached Sylvia, and she was whisked away for another dance.

Angry and frustrated, Robert turned and walked into a nearly empty saloon and ordered a whiskey.

Joey was having a difficult time falling asleep. Her thoughts were with Cavill, wondering where he was and if he was injured, alive, or dead.

She worried that he might be unhappy on the ranch after being a lawman for so long. She worried he would grow bored with the life of a rancher and seek to return to fighting for excitement, or worse, another woman.

She could tolerate his fighting, but not another woman.

Her bedroom door was open and Joey heard the faint sound

of tiny footsteps. Joey turned and peered through the dark and saw the tiny figure of Sarah.

"What are you doing out of bed?" Joey said softly.

"I had a bad dream," Sarah said. "I'm scared. Can I sleep with you?"

Joey pulled back the covers. "Just tonight," she said.

Sarah got in beside Joey and Joey hugged the child until both fell asleep.

After six or seven shots of whiskey, Robert fell asleep at a table and didn't stir until the bartender woke him up.

"Young fellow, time to go home and sleep it off," the bartender said.

Robert opened his eyes and said, "I have to get back to the dance."

"Son, the dance ended two hours ago," the bartender said.

Chapter Fifty

Nearly every citizen in Fort Smith lined both sides of Main Street as Reeves, Porter, and Witson led their group along the long street to the courthouse.

Judge Parker watched from the window of his office.

As the group dismounted at the courthouse steps, Reeves, Witson, and Cochran escorted Blue Duck and the Banjo brothers into holding cells in the basement of the courthouse.

"Let's go see the judge," Porter said.

When Trent discovered that his daughter didn't return home from the cotillion, he took the buggy to town to find out why.

People were still cleaning the streets when he arrived, and he stopped off to see the sheriff.

"My daughter didn't come home last night," Trent said. "The Creed boy escorted her and—"

"Robert Creed? He's sleeping it off out back," the sheriff said.

"What?" Trent said.

Porter, Duffy, Cavill, Goodluck, and Rajan joined Parker in his office.

"Rajan, how is the old chief?" Parker said.

"He is in good spirits," Rajan said.

"Tell him I was asking about him," Parker said. "And take him a box of my best cigars."

"I will," Rajan said.

"What did the Banjo brothers do that you picked them up on the way?" Parker said.

"They jumped Marshal Witson. We had no choice but to kill one of them," Porter said.

"Those boys were destined to hang," Parker said.

There was a knock on the door, it opened, and Reeves stepped in.

"Bass, bring Blue Duck to my courtroom," Parker said.

Seated on the jail cell cot, Robert looked up at Trent and the sheriff.

"I don't know what happened," Robert said. "She kept dancing with different fellows all night. I tried to stop her, but she just laughed at me. I got frustrated and went to the saloon for a drink. Next thing I know, I woke up and the dance was over."

"One of my deputies found him wandering the streets at two in the morning, calling her name," the sheriff said.

"Jesus Christ," Trent said.

"Now take it easy, Mr. Trent. I'm sure she'll turn up," the sheriff said.

A deputy appeared behind the sheriff.

"Sheriff, you better come to the livery right away," the deputy said.

In handcuffs and leg irons, Blue Duck stood before Judge Parker's bench in the courtroom.

Porter, Reeves, Cochran, Duffy, Cavill, and Goodluck sat in the first pew.

"Prisoner Blueford Duck, you will be given a fair trial and judged by a jury of your peers," Parker said. "And when you are found guilty of the attempted murder of Joseph Goodluck, I will sentence you to the maximum of twenty-five years without parole. You will die an old man in prison. Forgotten by all. Remembered by none."

"You will let me go this very day," Blue Duck said.

"And why would I do that?" Parker said.

"Knowledge," Blue Duck said. "I have it. You want it. We will make a bargain for it."

"Knowledge of what?" Parker said.

"These men who hunted me in Wyoming Territory want to know why I killed on the full moon," Blue Duck said. "Because I was paid to do so."

"By whom?" Parker said.

"That knowledge is not free," Blue Duck said.

"What do you want?" Parker said.

"I want to walk out of here and ride a horse out of your town," Blue Duck said. "In exchange for my freedom, I will give you the man who paid me to kill those people."

"Marshals Reeves and Cochran, return the prisoner to his cell," Parker said.

When the sheriff climbed the ladder to the loft of the livery stable, he was shocked to see the dead body of Sylvia Trent.

The sheriff was unaware that Trent followed him up the ladder until Trent started screaming behind him.

Trent rushed to Sylvia and grabbed her.

"No. Jesus God, no!" Trent screamed.

The sheriff could do nothing except watch Trent have a complete, total breakdown.

Parker sat behind his desk with a glass of whiskey and puffed on a cigar.

Porter, Duffy, Cavill, and Goodluck sat in chairs and waited.

"We have us a situation," Parker said. "On one hand, I have in my jail a vile and murderous criminal who will be found guilty and sentenced to twenty-five years. And on the other hand, without Blue Duck giving us the man responsible for the murders in Wyoming, that man lives to do it again. The question is, what do I do about it?"

Porter sighed and then stood up. "Judge, the man in Wyoming who paid Blue Duck, he will find another hired killer and continue unless he is stopped. We can't stop him unless we know who he is."

"Mr. Duffy, what do you say?" Parker said.

"I agree with Mr. Porter," Duffy said.

"Mr. Cavill?" Parker said.

"As much as it goes against the grain, I have to agree," Cavill said.

"Mr. Goodluck?" Parker said.

"Men like Blue Duck will commit more crimes and will be caught again," Goodluck said. "It's his destiny."

"I agree," Parker said.

"What's the matter with him?" the sheriff said to the town doctor.

"A fancy squirt of a doctor back east would say he's had a nervous breakdown," the doctor said. "The sight of seeing his daughter like that was just too much for him, I'm afraid."

"His daughter, what killed her?" the sheriff said.

"Strangulation," the doctor said.

The sheriff took a deep breath. "Was she violated?" he said.

"Yes," the doctor said. "Repeatedly."

"What do you mean repeatedly?" the sheriff said.

"By more than one man, would be my guess," the doctor said.

"My good God," the sheriff said.

"Sheriff, I'm just a country doctor, but I'll tell you this. God had nothing to do with what happened to that girl," the doctor said.

Blue Duck stood before Parker's bench as Reeves and Cochran stood directly behind him.

"Blueford Duck, in exchange for the information you claim to possess, I will meet the terms of your request," Parker said. "On one condition: that it is verified by Mr. Porter. You will remain in custody until Mr. Porter informs me that the man who hired you is in custody. At that time, you will walk out of here a free man."

"How long?" Blue Duck said.

Parker looked at Porter. "Mr. Porter, how much time do you need?"

"Thirty days should do it," Porter said.

"Blueford Duck, is that agreeable to you?" Parker said.

"Yes," Blue Duck said.

"Marshals Reeves and Cochran, get him cleaned up and then bring him to my office," Parker said.

Chapter Fifty-One

Dunstable Township was a very small town with seemingly nothing going for it except the woolen mill.

That was her first impression when Miss Potts stepped down from the rented buggy.

It was two in the afternoon, and not a soul stirred on the streets.

"I think everybody is at work at that mill," a deputy said.

"Not everybody," Miss Potts said.

She started walking to a wood building that had a sign over the door reading Town Hall.

The deputies followed, and together they entered the building.

A woman was seated behind a desk.

"Are you the mayor?" Miss Potts said.

"I'm the town clerk," the woman said.

"Is the mayor in?" Miss Potts said.

"The mayor is at the mill along with everyone else in this town," the woman said.

"I see," Miss Potts said. "Well then, maybe you can help us. The marshals and I are looking for a Mr. J. Frazier."

"Old Jake? What for?" the woman said.

"Is Mr. Frazier at the mill?" Miss Potts said.

"I'm not sure I should say where Mr. Frazier is," the woman said.

"These gentlemen are United States Marshals," Miss Potts

said. "We could be back in twenty-four hours with federal warrants to close the mill. Or, you could get Mr. Frazier for us. Which would you prefer?"

Cleaned up and wearing new pants and shirt, a shackled Blue Duck stood before Parker's bench in the courtroom. Witson and Reeves stood directly behind him.

"Blueford Duck, I have decided to accept your terms," Parker said.

"In writing," Blue Duck said.

"Yes, in writing," Parker said. "Now tell us the name of the man who hired you and why."

"The why is his business," Blue Duck said. "His name is Frazier, and he claims to be from Wyoming. But I know better. He's from back east somewhere. I can hear the twang of an eastern dude in his voice."

"How did you meet?" Parker said.

"He's in the cattle business, or so he claims," Blue Duck said. "Last fall, I was riding south from Canada to winter in Arkansas and Texas. It was a chance encounter on the Nebraska prairie. His buggy had broken a wheel when he was on his way to Wyoming. I happened by. I was going to rob and kill him, but instead he told me I was just the man he was looking for."

"How so?" Parker said.

"He said he wanted to shake things up in Wyoming Territory," Blue Duck said. "He said he would pay me one thousand dollars for every scalp I took from a white man on the full moon."

"Did he say why he wanted you to do this?"

"All he said was that Wyoming owed him," Blue Duck said. "I would kill white men for free, so to be paid to do it was what you call a bonus."

"He paid you, how?" Parker said.

"He gave me ten thousand dollars in advance," Blue Duck said. "I rode with him and waited on the Nebraska side of Cheyenne by this little creek. He returned within an hour and gave me the money. He told me he would pay me every month if I killed whites during the full moon. It was my pleasure to do so."

"What did he mean by 'Wyoming owed him'?" Parker said.

"You'd have to ask him," Blue Duck said. "He paid me to do his killing, not write a book about it."

"You said J. Frazier wasn't his real name. Why do you think that?" Parker said.

"I saw his leather wallet," Blue Duck said. "It had his initials in gold lettering. B.F., in bright gold. If your name was J. Frazier, would you have the initials of B.F. on your wallet?"

Duffy looked at Cavill and Goodluck.

"What did this man look like?" Parker said.

"Tall, thin, graying hair," Blue Duck said. "Maybe fifty or so. I'd recognize him for sure."

"As part of our agreement, I'll ask you to identify him when he is apprehended," Parker said.

"My pleasure," Blue Duck said.

"Mr. Porter, are you satisfied?" Parker said.

"For now," Porter said.

"Marshal Reeves, Cochran, escort Blue Duck back to his cell," Parker said.

Once Blue Duck was escorted out of the courtroom, Duffy said, "Mr. Porter, there is a prominent rancher named Ben Foster north of Cheyenne," he said. "He supposedly pulled out over the killings. He fits the description. He could be our man."

"Judge Parker, you'll hold Blue Duck until we check this out and send you a telegram?" Porter said.

"He'll sit in that cell until you wire me otherwise," Parker said.

"Name is John, but everybody in town calls me Jake," Frazier said.

Miss Potts stared at Frazier for a long moment. He was around sixty, with a graying beard and hair and wore spectacles. She found it difficult to believe that this J. Frazier could have masterminded such a vile plot.

"Mr. Frazier, have you ever been to Phoenix?" Miss Potts said.

"Phoenix? Where is that?" Frazier said.

"It's in Arizona," Miss Potts said.

"I never been west of the Ohio River," Frazier said.

"I see," Miss Potts said.

"Course, my cousin, now there's a traveling man," Frazier said. "Been out west more than thirty years, he has."

"Your cousin?" Miss Potts said.

"Ben. Ben Foster," Frazier said. "He left here thirty years ago and never looked back. He wanted me to go with—"

"Thank you, Mr. Frazier," Miss Potts said. "I appreciate your time."

Outside the town hall, Miss Potts said, "We have to get to Harrisburg as quickly as possible and catch a train to Cheyenne."

"Thank God for small favors," a marshal said.

As they waited on the platform for the train, Porter said, "This Ben Foster, what is his motive for devising such a plot?"

"Couldn't say at this time, Mr. Porter," Duffy said.

"Can Blue Duck be trusted?" Porter said.

"Of course not," Duffy said. "But he didn't pull the name Ben Foster and his description out of his hat. We've met Foster, and the description fits."

Porter looked at his watch. "We have time for me to wire Hale and let him know we're returning to Cheyenne," he said.

Chapter Fifty-Two

The sheriff stopped by the doctor's office to check on Trent's condition.

The news wasn't good.

"If he doesn't improve in a few days, I'm going to send him to the clinic in Colorado where they treat patients with mental trauma," the doctor said.

"I hate to hear that," the sheriff said.

"Any ideas on who killed the poor girl?" the doctor said.

"There were five hundred people at that dance, including trail hands passing through and strangers," the sheriff said. "I don't even know where to begin."

"The Creed boy came by this morning," the doctor said. "He's devastated by what happened."

"Maybe I'll go have another talk with him," the sheriff said.

As the train raced toward Cheyenne, Miss Potts and the marshals had breakfast in the dining car.

Miss Potts had her stack of reports from the series of murders. She flipped through the pile and removed one.

"Here it is," she said. "Ben Foster. A prominent rancher who sold his place after several of his men were murdered. Adcock and Charles died trying to track who committed the murders. Governor Hale stated that Foster came to Wyoming before the war and helped settle the land and make it a territory."

"Say that none of this is coincidence," a marshal said. "Say this Ben Foster is behind it all. What's his motive for all of it?"

"We can worry about that later, after he is caught," Miss Potts said. "Right now we have to get to Cheyenne and reach Mr. Porter."

Porter, Duffy, Cavill, and Goodluck had dinner in the dining car as the train sped to Cheyenne.

"What do we know about Ben Foster?" Porter said.

Duffy and Cavill knew from experience that Porter was seeking a motive for the crimes. By learning about Foster, the motive might become visible.

"He came to Wyoming when it was open, lawless country," Duffy said. "He fought Indians, cattle thieves, rustlers, and worse to build his ranch and make a go of it."

"Goodluck, you met him most often. What's your opinion?" Porter said.

"His wife died, and he has a young daughter," Goodluck said. "He didn't strike me as the sort of man to run at the sign of trouble."

"But yet, isn't that what he did?" Porter said. "Sell his ranch and run, rather than stay and fight."

"This man came to Wyoming before most of it was settled," Duffy said. "A man like that doesn't give up so easily unless . . ."

"Unless what?" Porter said.

"Unless that's what he wants us to think," Duffy said.

"That doesn't tell us his motive though," Porter said.

"Why would he want us to think he gave up and moved away?" Porter said.

"Remove suspicion from himself," Cavill said. "The mark of an amateur."

"True enough, Mr. Cavill," Porter said. "And like all

amateurs, he will have left something behind that will trip him up."

Miss Potts checked the train schedule before going to sleep. The next available train was scheduled to arrive in Cheyenne at ten in the morning.

She had a long list of things to do when the train arrived.

Top of the list was to find Mr. Porter.

Porter, Duffy, Cavill, and Goodluck had brandy and cigars in the gentlemen's car after dinner.

"We arrive in Cheyenne at noon," Porter said. "First thing we do is see the governor. Then we'll see Miss Potts and find out what progress she's made. She must be bored out of her mind by now."

Chapter Fifty-Three

It was a shock to the doctor when Trent opened his eyes and called for Sylvia. The doctor rushed to his side.

"Sylvia," Trent cried out.

"Now you just take it easy, Mr. Trent," the doctor said.

"Where is she?" Trent said.

"She's gone, Mr. Trent. You know that," the doctor said.

"Who did it? Who did that to my Sylvia?" Trent said.

"We don't know," the doctor said. "The sheriff is doing everything possible to find out."

"I need to send a telegram," Trent said.

"To whom?" the doctor said.

"James Duffy," Trent said.

"All right," the doctor said. "I'll have the telegraph operator stop by."

Varnell read the telegram from J. Frazier. It requested the bank close his account and have all funds wired to the First Bank of Omaha, in Nebraska.

It was a perfectly legal request and transaction, yet Varnell hesitated. Instead, he sent a telegram to Miss Potts at the Illinois Detective Agency in Springfield.

He decided to wait for a response from Miss Potts before transferring the funds.

Miss Potts and the deputies raced from the train depot to

Governor Hale's office the moment the train reached Cheyenne.

She was surprised to find that Porter, Duffy, Cavill, and Goodluck were on a train and wouldn't arrive until noon.

She couldn't wait to make her report, so she gave Hale every scrap of information she and the marshals had gathered.

"Ben Foster? I find that rather difficult to believe," Hale said.

"So did we, but it all links together," Miss Potts said.

"Why would Ben Foster hire a man like Blue Duck to murder innocent people every full moon?" Hale said. "It makes no sense, no sense at all."

"Governor, where is Mr. Porter?" Miss Potts said.

"He should be here within the hour," Hale said.

"Do you know where Ben Foster went after leaving Wyoming?" Miss Potts said.

"No," Hale said. "He didn't make that information known."

"He sold his ranch to Dunstable Incorporated, a company he owns," Miss Potts said. "There is no doubt of that."

Hale looked at his marshals. "What say you, gentlemen?"

"We've been with Miss Potts since we left Cheyenne," a deputy said. "We believe her to be one hundred percent correct."

Hale sighed. "God, what a mess," he said.

Hale and Miss Potts were just sitting down to lunch when Porter, Duffy, Cavill, and Goodluck arrived.

"Governor, we have every reason to believe that a man named Ben Foster is behind all this," Porter said.

"Sit down, Charles," Hale said. "Have lunch. Miss Potts has something to tell you."

During lunch, Miss Potts made her report to Porter, and Porter added his own report to Hale. "Miss Potts, it appears I underestimated your abilities all these years," Porter said.

"Thank you, sir," Miss Potts said.

"Governor, I believe we can have a countrywide bulletin put out for the arrest of Ben Foster," Porter said.

"Hopefully he hasn't left the country," Hale said.

There was a knock on the dining room door.

"Enter," Hale said.

An aide opened the door and walked to the table. "A telegram from Springfield," he said.

Porter held out his hand.

"It's addressed to Miss Potts," the aide said.

While Duffy and Cavill grinned, Miss Potts took the telegram and read it quickly.

"Ben Foster is in Omaha, Nebraska, and requested his funds be transferred from the Bank of Phoenix," she said.

"Governor, can your train take us to Omaha?" Porter said.

"It can," Hale said.

"Reply to the bank in Phoenix to wire Foster's funds in twenty-four hours," Porter said.

The aide nodded.

"How soon can your train be ready, Governor?" Porter said.

"When do you want to leave?" Hale said.

Porter looked at Duffy, Cavill, and Goodluck. "Let's go pack our gear," he said.

Duffy cleared his throat. Porter looked at him. "What?" Porter said.

"Miss Potts has earned her spurs, don't you think?" Duffy said.

"Pack your bags, Miss Potts," Porter said. "You'll be going with us."

Miss Potts smiled. "Yes, sir," she said.

CHAPTER FIFTY-FOUR

Duffy and Goodluck, dressed as cowboys, sat in chairs on the boardwalk outside the saloon and drank coffee.

Goodluck smoked a cigar. Duffy whittled on a stick.

Across the street at the First Bank of Omaha, Cavill stood inside, dressed as a bank guard, and kept watch at the window.

In the lobby of the Omaha Hotel, Porter and Miss Potts, dressed as a business couple, sat at a comfortable sofa and sipped coffee.

Also in the lobby, at another table, were a US Marshal and a deputy.

Nobody moved or seemed to notice as Ben Foster came down a flight of stairs wearing a suit and strolled across the lobby to the street.

As soon as Foster crossed the street, Porter, Miss Potts, the marshal, and the deputy stood and went to the lobby door.

In front of the saloon, Duffy and Goodluck watched as Foster crossed the street and walked to the bank,

In the bank, Cavill opened the door for Foster as the man entered. Then Cavill stood against the wall as Foster went into the bank manager's office.

Foster was in the manager's office for about twenty minutes. When he exited the office, he walked to the door. Cavill opened the door and Foster stepped out and into the arms of the US Marshal.

"Ben Foster, you're under arrest," the marshal said.

In the office in Springfield, the clerk monitoring Porter's private telegraph took a message from the telegraph station in Miles City.

"Oh, my God," he said as he read the text back to himself.

Then he began the response with, *Mr. James Duffy . . .*

Foster's daughter, Amelia, was allowed to ride on Hale's private train to Cheyenne, but in a car separate from her father's.

In the first riding car, Foster sat in a chair and sipped coffee. Duffy, Cavill, Goodluck, and Miss Potts sat at the table in the center of the car and ate a light dinner as the train sped to Cheyenne.

Porter lit a cigar and sat opposite Foster.

"Two dozen men, women, and children were killed. Two of them worked for me, and for what?" Porter said. "A wealthy, successful rancher, and for what?"

Foster looked at Porter. "I came to Wyoming when it was a savage wilderness," he said. "Before the railroad, before Cheyenne, before it became civilized. I fought the Cheyenne rustlers, murderers, and the lot. I buried my wife and lost my oldest son and raised my daughter alone. I helped make Wyoming what it is today."

"No one is belittling what you did, Mr. Foster," Porter said.

"It was bad enough when Grant appointed that idiot Campbell governor in sixty-nine," Porter said. "Last year, I applied for the appointment and was passed over by that buffoon Arthur. Me, one of the first ranchers in the entire territory, passed over for that pipsqueak Hale. It was too much for my soul to endure."

"You orchestrated this entire scheme because you were passed over for the position of territorial governorship?" Porter said.

"By all rights, I should be governor," Foster said. "If any man earned the right to take Wyoming to statehood, it's me."

Porter puffed on his cigar and stared at Foster in amazement.

"Maybe now Garfield will appoint me governor," Foster said. "Maybe now he'll listen."

"Well, you'll certainly get your say," Porter said. "I guarantee you that."

Foster smiled. "You think so?" he said. "Maybe I should write Arthur a letter? Would you have paper and pen?"

"Sure," Porter said.

"He can't refuse me now, can he?" Foster said.

"Miss Potts, could you get Mr. Foster some paper and pen?" Porter said.

"Perhaps you could endorse my letter to Arthur," Foster said. "Tell him everything I've done for Wyoming."

"I'm sure he already knows, Mr. Foster," Porter said.

EPILOGUE

"He's insane," Hale said. "There is no other word for it."

Porter, Duffy, Cavill, Goodluck, and Miss Potts were having dinner in Hale's private residence.

"Yes, I think it's safe to say insane is the word, all right," Hale said.

"He's been seething with rage since sixty-nine when he was passed over by Grant," Porter said. "That rage has slowly driven him mad, I'm afraid. Not being given the governorship by Arthur just drove him over the edge. His mind, his pride, could no longer conceive those he deemed to be inferior individuals being awarded what he felt was rightfully his."

"Not so mad he couldn't devise a brilliant plan to hold the entire territory hostage for nearly a year," Hale said.

"Madness and brilliance often walk hand-in-hand, I'm afraid," Porter said. "History is littered with brilliant, insane people."

There was a knock on the door. An aide opened the door and stepped inside with a telegram.

"For Mr. Duffy," the aide said.

He handed the envelope to Duffy, who tore it open and read it quickly.

All color drained from Duffy's face as he stood up and dropped the telegram.

"I have to go," Duffy said. "I have to go right now."

"Jim, what is it?" Cavill said.

Duffy rushed from the room, nearly knocking the aide to the floor on the way out.

"Mr. Duffy," Porter said.

Miss Potts picked up the telegram and read it quickly.

"Oh . . . my . . . God," she said as the telegram slipped through her fingers.

ABOUT THE AUTHOR

Ethan J. Wolfe is the author of a dozen historical western novels, including the popular series, The Regulator.

The employees of Five Star Publishing hope you have enjoyed this book.

Our Five Star novels explore little-known chapters from America's history, stories told from unique perspectives that will entertain a broad range of readers.

Other Five Star books are available at your local library, bookstore, all major book distributors, and directly from Five Star/Gale.

Connect with Five Star Publishing

Visit us on Facebook:
https://www.facebook.com/FiveStarCengage

Email:
FiveStar@cengage.com

For information about titles and placing orders:
(800) 223-1244
gale.orders@cengage.com

To share your comments, write to us:
Five Star Publishing
Attn: Publisher
10 Water St., Suite 310
Waterville, ME 04901